MAGIC & MISCHIEF

STARRY HOLLOW WITCHES, BOOK 3

ANNABEL CHASE

RED PALM PRESS LLC

Magic & Mischief

Starry Hollow Witches, Book 3

By Annabel Chase

Sign up for my newsletter here http://eepurl.com/ctYNzf **and like me on** Facebook **so you can find out about new releases**.

Cover Design by Alchemy

❀ Created with Vellum

CHAPTER 1

"EMBER, I think it's high time you attend your first meeting as a trustee of the Rose Foundation," Aunt Hyacinth said.

We sat in the sun parlor of the main house, sipping fizzlewick martinis. I felt very sophisticated drinking out of a glass instead of a bottle. Aunt Hyacinth was draped in one of her infamous kaftans, this one lavender covered with images of her white horse. Precious, her fluffy familiar, sat on her lap purring softly.

"The Rose Foundation?" I queried. "What's that?"

"One of the most generous charitable organizations in Starry Hollow," she said. "It was started by my grandparents. Each member of the family is on the Board of Trustees— except the children, of course—until they come of age. It's time for you to learn what being a Rose means in this town."

So far it seemed to mean bulldozing my way through bureaucracy and red tape and being told I lacked their typical ethereal beauty. I was eager to see what else it meant.

"Just tell me where and when."

"We meet right here at Thornhold, in the boardroom."

Why did it not surprise me that the house came equipped

with a boardroom? I bet there was also a bowling alley and a disco somewhere in the vast space she called home.

"We have a presentation today, so it will be a good opportunity for you to get your broomstick off the ground," Aunt Hyacinth said.

"There's flying involved?" I asked.

She stroked the cat. "No, darling. It's an expression. I believe humans say things like 'getting your feet wet.'"

Oh, that made sense. "What kind of presentation is it?"

My aunt waved a hand airily. "Other charitable organizations are always seeking money from us to fund their good works," she said. "Think of us as the bank and they spend the money, honey."

"Okay, I'll be there," I said.

"Make sure you wear something suitable," my aunt said, giving me the once-over.

"Like a kaftan?" I quipped before I could stop myself. I waited for a breathless moment to see how she responded. My time as a beloved Rose could be over in a millisecond.

"I might have something in your size," she said, completely serious. "I'm just not sure how I would feel about you wearing images of my companions. They're very personal to me."

"Well, I wouldn't dream of making you uncomfortable," I said, inwardly sighing with relief. "I'm sure I can find something in my own closet."

I arrived for the meeting ten minutes early because Florian warned me not to be late. The boardroom was located at the back of the stately home, a few rooms down from my aunt's office. The family sat around a large mahogany table. My cousins were present and accounted for, speaking to a short, squat man in a bowtie. His brown beard was packed with coarse hair and his long bushy mane was tied back in a ponytail.

"Oh, good," Aster said. "Here's our newest trustee now." She waved me over. "Ember Rose, I'd like you to meet our speaker this evening. This is Milo Jarvis, the president of Big Dreams."

I crossed the room to shake his hand. "Nice to meet you, Mr. Jarvis." He had to be a dwarf. He was too wide and hairy to be a leprechaun and too human-looking to be a troll.

Simon, my aunt's butler, entered the room with a tray of refreshments and set them on a sideboard.

"Fabulous," Aunt Hyacinth said. "Thank you, Simon." As imperious as she was, I noticed that she always thanked her staff. She could teach me a thing or two about manners, that was for sure.

"Everybody grab a drink, and we can get started," Florian said.

Just as everyone settled in their chairs and Milo took his place at the front of the room, the boardroom door swung open to reveal Wyatt Nash. He wore ripped jeans and a T-shirt that read *Keep Calm, I'm a Werewolf.*

Linnea made a sound of displeasure. "Wyatt, what do you think you're doing here?"

"There's a board meeting. Why wouldn't I be here?" The werewolf sauntered into the room and took the empty seat beside me.

"Since when do you take an interest in the activities of the Rose Foundation?" Aunt Hyacinth asked. "You didn't even take an interest when you were married into the family."

Wyatt placed his feet up on the table and rested his hands behind his head. "I'm acting as my children's representative until they come of age. Listen, I was perfectly happy to hang out at the Wishing Well and drink a few ales, but Hudson said there was a meeting. What kind of father would I be if I didn't show up for my kids?"

I could hear Linnea grumbling under her breath.

"As long as you sit here and remain silent, you are welcome to stay," Aunt Hyacinth said.

"Mother!" Linnea said, her cheeks burning.

"Technically, he is permitted to be here," Aunt Hyacinth said. "As long as he conducts himself in a gentlemanly manner, such as removing his feet from this two-hundred-year-old table, then I'm inclined not to make a fuss."

Wyatt dropped his feet to the floor and straightened in his chair. He even folded his hands in front of him for good measure. I half expected a halo to appear above his head, cartoon style.

Aunt Hyacinth nodded to Mr. Jarvis. "I apologize for the interruption. Why don't you get started, Milo?"

Milo tugged on his bowtie. I could see beads of sweat forming on his brow. I didn't blame him. Public speaking wasn't my thing either.

"Thank you for having me today," Milo said. "For those of you who don't know me, my name is Milo Jarvis and I'm the president of Big Dreams. We're a charity that supports families in times of need or crisis. For example, we recently sent the Gunnar family on vacation to Mistfall. The father, Bjorn, is terminally ill and it was the last chance for the family to spend time together and develop happy memories to last a lifetime."

I'd heard of charities like that in the human world. What I wouldn't give for the opportunity to have more good memories of my father or Karl, my husband. Of course, in my case, their deaths were sudden and unexpected. There was no chance for quality time or a long goodbye.

"We have fundraisers every year to raise money to continue our good works," Milo continued, "but it's foundations like yours that provide the bulk of the funding." He cleared his throat, clearly trying to quell his nerves. I wasn't sure whether he was always this nervous when presenting or whether it was the intimidating presence of the Rose family. Aunt Hyacinth's hospitality didn't fool anybody. She was a steel magnolia, as the southerners liked to say.

As Milo moved to start the video, the laptop he was using disappeared.

And so did his clothes.

For a full thirty seconds, nobody reacted. I think we were all in shock, including Milo Jarvis. He stood there in all his dwarf glory, buck naked. At least he was short enough that the top of the table obscured a view of his lower half. His private parts remained, thankfully, private.

Aunt Hyacinth was the first to gather her wits. "Milo, what is the meaning of this?"

Milo's chubby hands flew to cover his exposed bits. His face turned bright red and he struggled to speak.

Beside me, Wyatt erupted in laughter. "I've heard of ways of attracting investors, but this seems a little extreme." He stood and peered over the edge of the table. "And I do mean little."

Linnea glared at him. "Wyatt, that's enough."

Milo scanned the room, presumably for his clothes, but there was no sign of them.

Aunt Hyacinth gesticulated and said, "*Vestitus.*"

In the blink of an eye, Milo was fully clothed again. While it wasn't the same outfit, no one really cared. We were all just relieved that he was once again appropriately covered.

I jumped to my feet. "Let me get you a drink, Mr. Jarvis." I grabbed a glass of water from Simon's tray and handed it to the embarrassed dwarf. He gulped it down and gave back the empty glass.

"I am... I'm so sorry," he sputtered. "I don't understand what happened."

Aunt Hyacinth took it in stride. "It's taken care of, Milo. Please go on. How much money do you need for the year?"

I returned to my seat, wholly impressed that Milo was able to pull himself together and provide the numbers. I would've been huddled in a corner, rocking back and forth like a lunatic. He managed to speak eloquently about upcoming fundraisers and wishes they hoped to grant within the next six months. It was hard to hear about the difficulties the families faced. Sick children. Sheltering from abuse. I didn't envy Milo. Even though he was able to provide these families with a sliver of light, it also meant he had to spend a lot of time glimpsing the darkness.

"Thank you, Milo," my aunt said. "We'll discuss your request and get back to you within a week."

He slung an empty computer bag over his shoulder. There was no sign of his laptop or his original clothes.

"Thank you so much. Again, my deepest apologies. It isn't every day your worst nightmare comes true." He gave an awkward laugh and hurried from the room.

Once he was safely out of earshot, Wyatt elbowed me. "So your first exposure to a dwarf was actual exposure. Lucky you."

"Wyatt, don't be horrible," Linnea said. Then she rolled her eyes. "What am I saying? You don't know how to be anything else."

"What do you think happened?" I asked no one in particular. "He's a dwarf, right? Can they do magic?"

Aunt Hyacinth sipped her cocktail. The witch seemed to have a drink for all occasions. "Not usually. Maybe someone was trying to sabotage his presentation."

"Like a rival charity?" Aster asked. "That seems unusually cutthroat for a nonprofit."

Aunt Hyacinth shrugged. "You should all be grateful that you're seated where you are. I had no escape from the view."

I suppressed a laugh.

"His unexpected nudity aside," Aster said, "I vote in favor of funding."

"I think he earned it," Wyatt said.

"I agree," Aunt Hyacinth said. "I recommend funding. Does anyone object?" She looked around the table. No one said anything.

"Perfect," she said. "I'll have Chester make the arrangements."

"Who's Chester?" I asked.

"He's the family accountant," Florian said. "If you ever need money in a pinch, Chester is the man to see."

Aunt Hyacinth gave her son a pointed look. "I believe you'll find that I am the woman to see first, followed by Chester."

Florian bowed his white-blond head. "Of course, Mother. That part is understood."

She cocked her head. "Is it? Because Chester informed me that you came to him earlier this week about a down payment on a boat."

Florian glanced around the room, shifting uncomfortably in his seat. "I think that's a conversation for another time."

Aunt Hyacinth drained her glass. "I don't know about that. I think your siblings deserve to know how their portion of the estate is being spent."

Wow. She was naming and shaming him in front of the whole family. Aunt Hyacinth had no qualms about shining the spotlight on her wayward son.

"Florian already has a boat," Aster pointed out.

"Yes, but this one is offered by a master craftsman," Florian said. "Custom. She's called The Laughing Princess."

Wyatt nodded his approval. "Sounds ideal to me. Let me know when and I'll come and hang out with you."

Linnea narrowed her eyes at her ex-husband.

"Florian, I must admit, I'm tired of seeing you lounging around like a vampire after a visit to the blood bank. Why don't you at least go work for one of these worthwhile charities? Make yourself useful for a change." Aunt Hyacinth looked thoughtful. "I'll tell you what. If you spend at least one month working for a Starry Hollow organization—really working—then I will permit you to buy the boat."

Florian's expression brightened. "You will?"

Aunt Hyacinth rang one of her silver bells. "I will. Maybe it's just a matter of getting into work mode again."

Aster and Linnea voiced their displeasure.

"Mother, this is ridiculous," Aster said. "Linnea and I work incredibly hard, and we don't expect such over-the-top handouts."

Simon appeared and began to collect the empty glasses.

"I am the head of this household and it's my decision," Aunt Hyacinth said firmly. "If this is how I choose to encourage my son, then so be it."

Florian resisted the urge to look smug. "Thank you, Mother. I won't let you down."

Aunt Hyacinth pursed her coral lips. "We'll see about that."

CHAPTER 2

IN THE OFFICE the next day, I couldn't resist telling my colleagues about Milo Jarvis and his special presentation.

Bentley, the elf who put the 'ass' in associate editor, looked mildly amused. "A dwarf on display? That gives a whole new meaning to shrinkage."

Tanya's palm rested against her chest. "Bentley, have a heart. "That poor dwarf. He must've been mortified." As usual, the office manager fairy showed more compassion than Bentley or me.

"I think anyone would have been mortified, except an exhibitionist," I said.

"Speaking of exhibitions," Bentley said, "I'm covering an art show at one of the local galleries this evening. It should be a well-attended event."

Tanya clapped her hands together. "Did you ask that delightful nymph to go with you?"

My radar switched on. "Bentley, are you pursuing a young lady?"

Tanya appeared only too happy to share the news. "He is,

indeed. Her name is Meadow. They met online. They've been chatting for weeks now on MagicMirror."

"What's MagicMirror?" I asked.

"A platform where you can connect with paranormals anywhere in the world," Tanya said. "I've reconnected with old school chums. It's been an absolute treat."

"How did you connect with Meadow?" I asked.

"We're in the same group," Bentley said reluctantly.

"Which group?" I asked. I could tell he didn't want me to know, which only made me more determined to find out. He really was the little brother I never had.

"Propheteers—a group for fans of Alec Hale," Tanya said.

My eyes lit up. "There are online groups for Alec's readers?"

Bentley looked embarrassed by the admission. "Tanya, I don't tell you these things so that you can share them with the FNG."

Tanya ignored him. "I've been encouraging him for ages to get out there and meet someone. He can't spend his formative years collecting dust in this office. We don't all have the longevity of Mr. Hale."

"I'm fascinated by this on many levels," I said, leaning my elbows on the desk. "Alec has a reader group on Magic-Mirror and Bentley is in it."

"There are several groups," Tanya said. "I'm in the one for fairies over fifty. We're very active."

I slapped my hands on the desk. "Okay, someone needs to set me up with a MagicMirror account. I read *The Final Prophecy*. I want to be a Propheteer."

Bentley scowled. "It's for serious readers only."

"I *am* a serious reader," I insisted. "In fact, I've moved straight on to book two."

"I'll help you set it up," Tanya said, much to Bentley's

dismay. "Alec will be so pleased. He likes me to update him on the numbers."

Bentley appeared surprised. "He does?"

Tanya giggled. "He pretends to be disinterested, but he's nosier than you think."

My mental gears were busy clicking away. "So Bentley, your first official date with Meadow will be tonight at the art gallery?"

"Yes," Tanya answered for him. She seemed more excited about this than he did. "He's going to wear a striped tie that she sent to him. That way she'll know it's him."

"And what did you send to her?" I asked.

Bentley hesitated. "A silk scarf with silver stars."

That would be hard to miss. Suddenly, attending an artsy event sounded like a really good idea.

"Can I go, too?" I asked.

"I'm afraid not," Bentley said. "Arts and culture is my beat."

"In that case, she can attend as my guest," a voice said. Alec Hale stood behind us. Despite his six-foot-two frame, he managed to move with complete silence. He made ninjas sound like clumsy elephants.

"I didn't realize you'd be attending as well," Bentley said.

"The artist is a friend of mine," he said. "I promised to show my support." He glanced at me. "It might also be an opportunity for Miss Rose to get to know more people in town. It's always a plus for the paper to have access to more sources."

"I'm tapped in to the cultural scene," Bentley whined.

"There's no harm in including Miss Rose," Alec assured him. "I have no doubt her aunt will be pleased with the decision."

"Good point," I said. "So, what do I wear to an art shindig?"

"Clothes," Bentley quipped. "Unlike Milo Jarvis."

We laughed and Alec gave us a quizzical look.

"Ember was just telling us about something that happened at the Rose Foundation board meeting," Bentley said, and relayed the story.

"How odd," Alec said.

"Milo was a good sport," I said. "He got through the rest of his presentation like a champ."

"Let's hope everyone manages to retain their clothes this evening," Alec said.

"Except Bentley," I said. "We want his date to go well."

The tips of Bentley's pointed ears burned bright red. "Please don't embarrass me in front of her."

I patted him on the shoulder. "Don't worry. I'll leave that part to you."

Marigold, the coven's Mistress-of-Psychic Skills, decided that our next lesson should take place in the woods behind the cottage.

"Is this a witch thing?" I asked. "Is this because we're supposed to love nature and all that?"

Marigold looked slightly amused. "Yes, and all that. Also, it's practical. There's plenty of space and no one to interrupt. Psychic skills take a lot of concentration and focus."

She wasn't wrong there. I seemed to feel more exhausted after a psychic skills lesson than after listening to Bentley drone on for an hour about the history of journalism.

"So what's on the agenda today?" I asked, rubbing my hands together. "Am I going to uproot a tree with my mind?" Telekinesis was apparently one of my strengths, so Marigold was tasked with helping me hone my skill.

"Why on earth would you want to uproot a tree?"

I shrugged. "Maybe if I'm being chased by an ogre?" I held up a finger. "Or a giant. Are they real?"

MAGIC & MISCHIEF

"Yes, ogres and giants are real. They tend to live in more rural areas, rather than a highly populated town like Starry Hollow."

I laughed. "You think this is highly populated? You haven't seen the Cherry Hill Mall at Christmastime."

Marigold ignored my comment. "Why don't you have a seat on that log and we'll get started?"

I did as instructed and folded my hands primly in my lap.

"We're going to try astral projection today. Do you remember what that is?"

I pressed my lips together. "It's when my consciousness leaves my body, right? So I can Casper my way around town?"

"Casper?" she queried.

"Like a ghost," I said.

"Yes, something like that," Marigold said. "Observe." She sat on the ground in front of me in a cross-legged position. Her eyes closed and she began to breathe deeply. The simple act of observing her stillness put me in a trancelike state. It was like getting lost in the face of a ticking clock. After a moment, she rose to her feet.

"What happened?" I asked. "You're giving up already? Not for nothin', Marigold, but that's not a very good lesson."

Marigold looked at me. Although her mouth moved, I couldn't hear any of the words. She moved to the left and it was then that I saw the figure slumped on the ground in front of me. Two Marigolds. Her brown corkscrew curls bounced like a Slinky as her body drifted to the side, finally toppling over. Ghost Marigold turned to look at her shell. Her mouth moved again, and I was pretty sure I saw her lips form an obscenity. She began to move around the woods, demonstrating her ability to move through objects like trees and bushes. She was impervious to Spanish moss. She really was like a ghost.

13

"My turn, my turn," I said, waving my hand in the air like an eager student. No teacher ever saw me behave like this in the classroom. School was the last place I'd wanted to be. That was one reason it was so difficult to wrap my head around the fact that I had an academic child like Marley. School was her favorite place in the world. A rocket launcher shot that apple as far from the tree as possible.

Ghost Marigold moved back toward her body and I watched as the apparitional form was sucked back into its case. Marigold sat up and opened her eyes. She wiped the dirt from her cheek.

"I was hoping to stay upright," she said. "Sometimes it doesn't quite work out."

"That was pretty cool," I said. "Why can't you talk?"

"It's your consciousness that you separated from your physical form," Marigold explained. "Your body has a voice, but not your astral plane form."

"Do you have to stay close to your body? What if you get lost and can't find your way back to it?" Something that would likely happen to me.

"There's an invisible link between the forms," Marigold said. "Your body will keep you within a certain range. You'll feel the tug on the psychic rope, if you will. If you do stray out of range, your body will snap you back. You need to be careful of that because it can really hurt." She rubbed her lower back, as though remembering such a time.

"And I'll be like a ghost? People will be able to see me, but not hear me?"

"That's correct," Marigold said. "But you also have the potential to interact with the physical world in your spiritual form."

I frowned. "How's that possible? I watched you walk through trees and moss."

"Because I willed it to be so," Marigold said. "You have

14

telekinetic ability. You use your will to control objects. Essentially, it's your will walking around outside of your body."

I tried to comprehend her words. "So if I want to pick up a stick in my ghost body, I can do that?"

"Or your wand," she said. "In the event that you're defending yourself."

"Wouldn't it just make more sense to defend myself in my physical body?" I asked. "Aren't I leaving it vulnerable if it's just slumped on the ground somewhere with no protection?"

Marigold smiled. "That's an excellent question, Ember. It is true that your body is very vulnerable when you're no longer occupying it. Some witches perform a protective spell in the body before projecting. It all depends on the situation."

"What's the point of it?" I asked. "You said I might want to use my wand in my defense, but I can't picture a situation where this would come in handy."

Marigold's expression turned grim. "And let's hope you never encounter one. Many of these skills are antiquated. They are simply abilities passed down from one generation to the next."

Another thought occurred to me. "When will I be able to get a wand of my own?" I didn't mention that I'd been practicing with Linnea's childhood wand over at Palmetto House. No need to throw my cousin under the bus.

Marigold studied me. "Do you think you're ready for a wand? You're taking on a lot as it is."

"I won't know if I'm ready until I try," I said.

"I'll speak to your aunt," Marigold said finally. "It's her decision."

"So if she says yes, will you bring me a starter wand for the next lesson?"

Marigold laughed softly. "Not me. I'm the Mistress-of-

Psychic Skills. It will be Wren Stanton-Summer, the Master-of-Incantation."

Right. The hot wizard from my first coven meeting. No surprise he was adept with a wand.

"Are you ready to try astral projection?" Marigold inquired.

"I guess so," I said. Truth be told, I was a little nervous about splitting my body into two parts. What if I couldn't rejoin them?

"You'll do great," Marigold assured me in her typical peppy fashion.

I glared at her. "Stay out of my head, please."

She crouched beside me. "Focus on your breathing first. That's the key. Then relax your body, one muscle at a time."

I squinted. "That's a lot of muscles."

She gave an exasperated sigh. "Just focus on the ones you know."

My body softened and I focused inward, willing my consciousness to shed its skin. I felt something shift inside me, and before I realized what was happening, the ghostly version of me was looking down at my physical body. It was…unnerving.

I glanced at Marigold, who gave me an eager thumbs up. I didn't know what to do next. She gestured for me to walk around and pointed to one of the live oaks. Ah, she wanted me to walk through it.

I took an imaginary breath and headed for the base of the tree. As my body moved through it, a gust of air seemed to fill me. It was a strange sensation, like a fan blowing inside me. I reached the other side of the tree and peered around the bend to see Marigold jumping up and down with excitement. She wasn't the most poised witch you'd ever met.

She gestured for me to return to my body. I was only too

happy to oblige. The whole experience felt unsettling. Hopefully, it wasn't a skill I'd need to display on a regular basis.

I rejoined my body and opened my eyes. "I feel stiff."

"Completely normal." Marigold pulled me to my feet and enveloped me in a hug. "You did it. Aren't you proud?"

"I guess."

"You guess?" She pulled back and examined me. "Ember, this is an amazing talent you have. Do you know how many witches and wizards wish they could astral project? You must embrace it."

"I'll do my best."

She patted my cheek. "That's all we ask."

CHAPTER 3

I'D NEVER BEEN to an art gallery before. The closest I had come was a trip to the art museum in Philadelphia in seventh grade. I still remembered the enormous painting of a man getting his liver eaten by a giant bird. When I'd mentioned the painting to Marley one time, she told me it was called *Prometheus Bound* by Peter Paul Rubens. Prometheus was a demigod who was being punished by Zeus for introducing fire to men. It had been a disturbing image to a thirteen-year-old girl. While most of the students had been giggling over statues of naked men and women, I'd been haunted by Prometheus and his daily torture. According to Marley, the liver grew back every day and Prometheus suffered at the beak of the bird anew.

"I'm glad Aster helped you choose an outfit for tonight," Marley said, admiring my red dress.

"What are you trying to say? That your mother doesn't have good taste?"

Marley flashed me an innocent look. "I'm just saying that your idea of a nice outfit is probably not art gallery ready."

I laughed. "You're lucky you're so cute." I twirled around

in front of the full-length mirror, appreciating the way the fabric clung to my curves. I wasn't the walking stick I used to be. I had to admit, though, I preferred this older body. It felt more womanly than the breastless beanpole I'd been before my pregnancy.

"I hope the date goes well," Marley said. "It's been such a long time since you've been on one. Maybe we should have brushed up on some articles first. Done our research on appropriate behavior."

I placed my hands on my hips. "Marley Rose, this is not a date. This is business. Alec invited me as part of my job."

Marley's brow lifted. "That's right. You call him Alec now. So is he calling you Ember?"

I hesitated. "No, not yet. After tonight, maybe he will."

"What makes you think that?" Marley challenged. "Because it's a date?"

I stuck out my tongue. "You are so funny." I scooped up a pair of earrings off the ledge of the sink and stuck them in my lobes. Although I rarely wore any jewelry, the red dress cried out for accessories.

"The earrings are a nice touch," Marley said. "Very sophisticated."

I swatted her arm. "Mrs. Babcock should be here any minute. I'm sure she would appreciate it if you went to sleep in your own bed."

"No," she said. "I'm sure *you* would appreciate it if I went to sleep in my own bed. Mrs. Babcock doesn't care either way."

"She cares," I lied. "She told me. She said ten-year-olds like Marley should absolutely, always, under all circumstances sleep in their own bed. True story."

Marley folded her arms. "Then we'll just have to ask her when she gets here."

ANNABEL CHASE

Popcorn balls. Outsmarted by my own daughter. Not that I was surprised. Marley started outsmarting me as a toddler.

The doorbell rang and we both jumped. PP3 leaped off the couch and went straight for the door.

"Do you think it's Alec?" I asked.

Marley shook her head. "It's Mrs. Babcock."

I frowned. "How do you know?"

"Because Prescott Peabody III isn't barking. He'd bark at a vampire, but he doesn't bark at Mrs. Babcock."

I opened the door and, sure enough, Mrs. Babcock stood on the front step. The petite brownie's white hair was pulled back in its usual bun and she wore her wire-rimmed glasses. Tonight she'd traded a plain brown dress for a dark green one.

"Good evening, Ember," she said, entering the cottage. "My, aren't you a vision. An art show, is it?"

"Yes, apparently they're fancy events. I was told to dress appropriately." I seemed to be told that a lot in Starry Hollow. I guess what was appropriate in New Jersey was deemed substandard for the paranormal town.

"Well, mark my words. You'll be taking attention away from the artwork looking like that," Mrs. Babcock said with a wink. "Not such a bad thing." She swept into the room and began unpacking her bag. It looked like a medical bag in size and shape, and I watched in fascination as she began to pull several board games from inside.

"How would you feel about Scrabble tonight?" Mrs. Babcock asked Marley.

"As long as we can play chess afterward," Marley said.

"It's a deal." Mrs. Babcock continued unloading her bags, including a plastic container of what I assumed were home-made cookies.

"Mrs. Babcock, how can you possibly fit all of that inside such a tiny bag?"

She gave me a Mona Lisa smile. "Whatever do you mean, Ember? This bag fits all my needs. I've had it since I was a young girl."

It was some kind of magic bag that seemed to have an infinite base. Women around the world could use a bag like that.

PP3 began to growl.

"Prescott Peabody, mind your manners," I scolded him.

Mrs. Babcock patted the dog on the head. "Don't worry, dear. He isn't growling at me."

A knock on the door proved her right. I opened the door and my breathing hitched. Alec Hale stood on the doorstep, looking more dashing than I'd seen him yet. You would think an evening at the art gallery would be no different for him. He was always impeccably dressed in a perfectly tailored suit. Tonight was different. Tonight, he wore a traditional tuxedo. My gaze was drawn to the green handkerchief in his pocket that matched the color of his eyes. Instead of slicked back, his golden blond hair was tousled.

"Miss Rose," he said. I noticed the twitch of his cheek. "You are…not wearing your usual clothes."

I smiled. "That's very observant for a journalist."

"I wasn't expecting a red dress," he said. "For some reason, I pictured you in black."

As I turned to fetch my bag, I felt his admiring gaze on my back.

"I did wear a lot of black in New Jersey," I said. "But Aster insisted I wear a pop of color, as she put it. I can't take any credit. She chose the red."

"It suits you," he said. His gaze lingered a beat too long and he seemed unsettled, not his usual cool and collected self. I made sure to shield my thoughts, so that he couldn't tell how handsome I thought he looked in his James Bond tuxedo.

"Shall we?" he asked, offering his arm.

I looped my arm through his and called over my shoulder, "Goodnight, ladies."

"Have fun, Mom," Marley said. "Try not to spill anything on your dress...or any of the artwork."

I closed the door behind me and was immediately confronted by a stretch limousine.

"Is this your usual ride?" I asked, stopping short.

"I tend to use it for special events, yes."

"I assume this is the result of bestselling author money and not editor-in-chief of a weekly paper in a small town money," I said. I didn't need to have worked in a newspaper office in the human world to know that they didn't make very much money.

"I am the editor-in-chief of *Vox Populi* because it is my passion," he replied. "My books aside, I am a vampire, Miss Rose. I have had many years to accumulate my wealth."

Harrumph. I guess he told me.

I slid into the backseat and rubbed my hands on the soft leather. It was like sitting on a cloud. Alec moved in to sit beside me, his thigh pressed against mine. As it was spacious in the backseat, his closeness surprised me, but it felt too good to pull away. I wondered whether our physical proximity was having the same effect on him as it was on me.

We arrived in front of the art gallery too soon and I tried not to show my disappointment. The driver opened my door first, followed by Alec's.

Despite the tuxedo, the event was even fancier than I expected, with a fully staffed bar and waiters circling the guests. Bentley was already there, hovering beside the bar. His flushed cheeks suggested he'd taken advantage of the free alcohol.

"Nice tie," I said, flicking the blue and green striped tie

with my fingers. "Any sign of your MagicMirror girlfriend yet?"

"None of your business," he snapped.

"Should you be getting sloshed if you're here to cover the show for the paper?"

He glared at me. "Why don't you go climb up our editor's butt where you clearly find it so comfortable?"

"Good one, Bentley." I held up my palm to high-five him, but he simply blinked. I lowered my hand and sighed. "What's the problem? Are you worried Mildew won't show?"

"Meadow," he corrected me. "What if she's awful? What if she looks nothing like her photo?"

"Do you look like your photo?" I asked.

Bentley straightened, indignant. "Of course. I use the one from the paper. I'm easy enough to verify." He peered into the crowd and stiffened. "Great goblins! I just saw a silk scarf with silver stars. She's here."

I thrust Bentley forward without a second thought. His body went completely rigid, which I assumed was due to nerves. He was finally meeting Meadow in person. Maybe after weeks of fantasizing, the reality was about to prove too overwhelming for him.

"No," he said softly.

"It's okay, Bentley," I said, urging him forward.

"No, no, no." He pushed backward, almost frantic.

"Crap on a stick, Bentley," I said, getting annoyed. "She's a nymph, not a goddess. A nymph who won't be interested if she thinks you're a wimp."

"Not a nymph," he said in a harsh whisper. He whipped around to face me. "Meadow's not a nymph."

I gripped him by the shoulders. "Bentley, relax. You're about to hyperventilate and I haven't got a brown bag handy."

His face drained of color. "Look."

I peered over his shoulder to catch a glimpse of Meadow. My jaw unhinged when I saw the creature wearing the scarf with the silver stars. It was nearly seven feet tall and hairier than Hugh Jackman's Wolverine. Even more disconcerting was the bright peach-colored lipstick and high heels the creature wore.

"Dear God. What is that thing?" I asked quietly.

"A yeti," Bentley said, close to tears. "Meadow isn't a nymph. She's a yeti." He began to gulp for air.

"Calm down," I said, rubbing his back. "Take a deep breath." I wasn't the best comforter in the world, especially to my office frenemy, but he was so distraught that I couldn't leave him like this.

"Why a yeti?" he whimpered. "Anything but a yeti."

"Okay, so she claimed to be a nymph. She probably thought that was more acceptable to an elf, right?" The size difference was appreciable, to say the least. If the yeti was feeling amorous, Bentley was likely to snap like a twig.

"I knew she was too good to be true," he said. "I told myself every day not to trust it."

"Trust what?"

"The connection between us." He buried his face in his hands. "We got along too well. She seemed perfect in every way. Of course it had to be an act."

"The yeti's coming this way," I said. "What do you want to do?"

He didn't give a verbal answer. Instead, he bolted from the gallery, circumventing the yeti completely.

"Can I get you anything to drink, miss?" the bartender asked.

I turned my attention toward him. "Your strongest ale would be great." I was going to need to drink the sight of the lipsticked yeti out of my mind.

Alec appeared beside me, smooth as the silk scarf around

the yeti's thick neck. "How are you enjoying the event, Miss Rose?"

"Better than Bentley," I said, guzzling the ale. "I think one of us will need to write the article on the show. He's fled the scene."

Alec arched a blond eyebrow. "Fled? Was he ill?"

"If mortified counts as an illness, then yes. His Magic-Mirror pen pal turned out to be a yeti. He escaped rather than confront the situation."

"A yeti?" Alec queried. "How does he know?"

"Because the yeti is here." I spun toward the crowd, nearly spilling my drink on Alec's expensive shoes. There was no sign of the enormous yeti.

Alec followed my gaze. "I am quite sure I would notice a yeti in the art gallery. They tend toward the taller side."

"Yes," I agreed. "This one is about seven feet tall wearing high heels, lipstick, and a silk scarf."

Alec laughed. "That sounds like the most attractive yeti in existence."

I stared into the crowd, wondering where the yeti went and how Alec could have missed it.

"Never mind Bentley and his adolescent drama. Come and meet Trupti," Alec said. "I think you'll find her delightful."

Trupti Kapoor was a tall woman with midnight black hair that hung loose across her shoulders. She wore a yellow dress that complemented her brown skin.

"Trupti, your artwork is thought-provoking as always," Alec said, giving her a kiss on each cheek. "I'd like to introduce the newest addition to the *Vox Populi* staff, Miss Ember Rose."

Trupti gave me an appraising look. "Red is your color, my love. It shows off the fire in your heart."

"Um, thanks," I replied. I guess that was the artsy way of saying I look nice.

"We'd love a personal tour of your work," Alec said. "Miss Rose is new to town and hasn't yet been exposed to the excellent talent we have here."

"Aren't you full of compliments tonight?" Trupti said, and batted her thick, dark lashes at him. Ooh, I was so envious of those lashes right now. Mine were like thin spiders and not even the good kind—more like the anemic spiders that no one bothered to step on because they were deemed too insignificant.

She walked toward the far wall and we kept pace with her long strides. It was easy for Alec, but I really had to hustle. She stopped in front of a huge painting on the wall of—a green pear? Huh. I was pretty sure Marley could paint this in an afternoon. I was glad I'd only had one glass of ale so far. Loose lips sank ships…and insulted artists.

"I see the attention to detail," Alec said, admiring it—or pretending to admire it. I couldn't tell which. The vampire was a smooth operator.

"If you don't mind me asking, what inspired you to paint a piece of fruit?" I asked. Okay, so I couldn't keep my mouth completely shut. That went against my nature.

"As you can see, much of this exhibit involves fruit," she said, gesturing to the walls. I noticed paintings of a banana, an orange, and an apple.

"Because you're a very, very healthy eater?" I asked.

Trupti laughed. "On the contrary. My parents were adamant that I eat healthy foods as a child. I hated fruit. They would sit me at the table and refuse to let me leave until I ate all my fruit."

"You didn't like any fruit at all?" I asked. Usually there was a preference for citrus or berries. Even Marley ate fruit and she was a notoriously picky eater.

Trupti shook her dark head. "I spent many a night at the table, falling asleep. I'd wake up to the image of fruit right in front of my eyes." She shuddered. "They haunted my dreams."

"And so you paint them?"

She inhaled deeply. "A reflection of my childhood trauma. The art helps me to exorcise those particular demons."

"Doesn't it make you focus on them more?" I asked.

Her brow creased. "It helps me bleed them from my system. I take them from my psyche and leave them on the canvas to rot."

Alrighty then.

"Miss Rose is no stranger to traumatic childhoods," Alec said, resting his hand gently on the small of my back. It felt nice. Comfortable even.

Trupti fixed her gaze on me. "Ah, but of course. I've heard your story."

"Probably not all of it, but that's okay," I said. "Maybe someone should sit me down with paint and a canvas and see what I come up with."

"I shudder to think," Alec said.

"I occasionally host a class," Trupti said. "Six-week sessions. I'll let you know the next time I have one."

"That would be great," I said. I nodded toward another set of paintings on the adjacent wall. "These are nice. Are they the result of trauma, too?"

There were six paintings side by side, each one with splashes of color in the shape of a ballerina. Think Jackson Pollock meets Edgar Degas.

"No, my love," Trupti said. "These are called Metamorphosis One through Six. They represent my transformation into a vampire."

"You were turned?" I asked. I knew from recent experience that some people were turned into vampires and others were born as one.

"I was." She clasped her hands in front of her and contemplated the paintings. "You can see my struggle from one image to the next."

Although I saw only lots of paint splotches, I held my tongue. The artwork was obviously of a very personal nature and I had no intention of being dismissive.

Trupti plucked a glass from a passing waiter. "I think it's some of my best work to date. I'm very proud."

"As you should be," Alec said. "They're stunning." *As are you, Miss Rose.*

I glanced quickly at my companion. Did I seriously just hear that? His expression remained neutral with the exception of his fangs poking out a smidge. Damn vampire face.

"Why don't I see your fangs?" I asked Trupti.

"I beg your pardon," Trupti said, taken aback.

"I always see Alec's fangs, so it's obvious he's a vampire, but I can't see yours. Do you shave yours down or something?"

A look passed between Trupti and Alec that I didn't understand.

"I don't shave mine," Trupti said, with a trace of amusement. "The mere idea of it makes my skin crawl."

"So his are just longer," I said. "A male versus female trait maybe?"

"Perhaps," Trupti said vaguely, and sipped her cocktail.

"We should let the artist mingle with her other guests," Alec said, his hand still on my back. "Do let us know how the evening turns out."

"Same to you, darling." She blew him a kiss and we walked away.

"Shall I escort you home?" Alec asked.

"I hope you do, since I didn't drive here," I said.

A smile tugged at his lips. "Right this way, Miss Rose."

We exited the gallery, my thoughts on poor Bentley.

"Bentley will be fine," Alec said, once we were in the back of the limo.

I shot him a disgruntled look. "You're not supposed to be able to read my thoughts."

"Your shield is weak tonight," he said. "From the alcohol."

"Well, so is yours. I know you think I look stunning," I said, and proceeded to burp in his face. Sweet baby Elvis. Kill me now.

To his credit, he ignored it like the vampire gentleman he was. "You do look stunning. It's not a secret. Everyone in the gallery thought so, except Bentley, of course."

I squinted. "You read their minds?"

He shrugged. "Not deliberately. Sometimes I catch snippets of thoughts. This evening, I caught many snippets about the woman in the red dress. And I must say, Miss Rose, I wholeheartedly agree."

I inched closer to him. "You can't tell me I look stunning and then call me Miss Rose."

He gazed down at me. "Why not?"

"Because it's such a personal comment," I argued. "But then you use my last name to maintain distance from me. That's Marley's theory anyway. It sends a mixed message." Sheesh. What was in that ale? My mouth was working overtime.

"Marley has a theory, does she?" His mouth twitched again in that way I found incredibly sexy. Damn vampire face.

"Damn and vampire do tend to go hand in hand," Alec said.

I groaned in frustration. "Why can I see your fangs so often? I get the sense that isn't normal."

"Oh, it's very normal," Alec said, his thigh pressed against mine again. The limo pulled in front of Rose Cottage and I simultaneously wanted to climb onto Alec's lap and jet inside the cottage.

"Because vampire fangs are normal?"

"Because I'm very attracted to you, Miss Rose," he said matter-of-factly.

Oh. Not the answer I was expecting.

"Well," I said, straightening beside him. "I guess I'm very attracted to you, too." Take that, Mr. Matter-of-Fact.

"But it cannot possibly go anywhere," he said. "And so I resist the temptation."

"Exactly, " I said, and then hesitated. "Wait. Why can't it go anywhere?"

He gave me a sad smile. "You are a Rose. A descendant of the One True Witch. Niece of my employer, the most powerful witch in Starry Hollow. Hyacinth would never approve of me as a suitor for her blood relation."

"But she adores you."

"She adores me in the role I play," he said. "If I attempted to climb out of my box...Well, she would not appreciate my efforts. Not with her niece. You see how she feels about Wyatt Nash."

"But Wyatt is a playboy werewolf whose idea of high fashion involves cowboy boots."

"It's more the werewolf part that bothers Hyacinth," he said. "If Wyatt had been a philandering wizard, your aunt would have gladly looked the other way."

"And she feels the same way about vampires?" I asked.

"She feels the same way about anyone that isn't a member of the coven, and even then there might be issues."

I paused. "Like my mother?"

He nodded somberly. "Exactly."

I stared at his handsome face. I longed to trace his rugged jawline with my finger.

"I'm sorry, Miss Rose," he said. "But let us try to enjoy the time we spend together, no matter the circumstances."

I sighed deeply. "I'll try, but I'd much rather enjoy the time we spend together in a variety of unholy positions."

He choked back a laugh. "Goodnight, Miss Rose. Pleasant dreams."

I remained rooted to the soft leather, unable to tear myself away from him.

"Go, before we do something we regret," he urged.

I took one last look at the handsome vampire who wanted me. It was both strange and remarkable.

"Goodnight, Alec," I said, and hurried toward the certainty of Rose Cottage.

CHAPTER 4

WREN STANTON-SUMMER WAS the Master-of Incantation and
my latest coven tutor. His fraternal twin brother, Dillon, was
the head of security for the coven, otherwise known as the
Watchman. The brothers also happened to be cousins of
Aster's husband, Sterling—ah, the tangled web of coven
relations.

Wren was prime wizard beefcake, a far cry from the
crazed clown and cheerleader-cum-drill sergeant I'd labored
under so far.

"Why did you want to meet here instead of the cottage?" I
asked. We stood in the heart of town, on the corner of
Thistle Road and Coastline Drive.

"Because we need to do a little shopping before we can
get started," Wren said.

"What kind of shopping? Is it time for my first pair of
colorful striped tights?"

"Not unless you want to look like Marigold," he said. He
looked me up and down. "I'm guessing that's not a life goal."

"Not really," I said. "I'm more of a minimalist."

Wren smiled. "Good. So am I." He turned and began to

walk down the block and I hurried to keep up with his brisk pace. He came to a halt in front of Spellcaster's and opened the door. A bell above us jingled, reminding me of Aunt Hyacinth's silver bells.

"What's in here that I need?" I asked. The shop was full of every magical item you could imagine. Brooms, pointy black hats, and ugly black shoes with buckles that reminded me of the Pilgrims.

"For starters, you need a wand," Wren said.

I bit my lip. I didn't want to tell him that I'd been practicing with Linnea's starter wand. I knew my aunt wouldn't like it and Linnea was desperate to keep her assistance secret. Nobody wanted to poke Aunt Hyacinth's nest.

"Okay," I said. "Let's go for it. What's the procedure?"

Wren strode down the aisle labeled 'basic wands.' "It's like buying the right baseball bat or golf club. You need to see what feels right for you."

"There's no magic to it? A wand isn't going to tap me on the shoulder and choose me? I'm not going to hear one calling to me?"

His brow wrinkled. "If you hear one talking to you, let me know so I can summon the healer because it means you're on the fast train to Delusion Town. Population: you."

Beefcake *and* sarcasm. In some circles, that would make him fairly irresistible, however, I tended to prefer the sarcasm be one-sided—my side.

"Good to know." I studied the wide array of wands on the shelves. There were so many choices, I didn't know where to look first. "I had no idea they came in so many colors."

"That's a newer trend," he said. "When I was a boy, all starter wands were black, brown, or white."

"Linnea had a red one," I said. In a case that resembled a large lipstick tube.

Wren cocked an eyebrow. "Did she? I suppose that's

because she's a Rose. Your family has access to things that the rest of us don't."

I laughed. "Then what am I doing here with you? What if I want special treatment?"

Wren's expression shifted. "Make no mistake, Ember. You're already getting it."

My smile faded. He was right. I knew perfectly well that I was receiving preferential treatment. My job at *Vox Populi*, my late entry to the coven, my individual tutoring—my aunt had gone above and beyond what she would've done for any normal witch. Then again, I would do the same for a beloved family member. I just didn't know I had anyone aside from Marley until my trio of cousins showed up in New Jersey.

"What about this one?" Wren queried, tapping a simple black wand on the shelf.

"I am partial to black," I said. Secretly though, I'd grown accustomed to Linnea's bright red wand and wondered whether a pop of color wouldn't be better.

"I'm sensing hesitation," Wren said. "No big deal. We can keep looking."

"Is there any advantage to having a black or brown wand?" I asked. "Or were Silver Moon witches and wizards just really boring back in the day?"

Wren chuckled. "Hey, I'm not that old. Linnea is only a couple years younger than me. You have to remember that our coven draws much of its magic from nature. Black, brown, and white are colors of earth."

"What about blue?" I asked. "Like the sky and the sea? Or green?"

Wren resisted a smile. "Okay, so maybe the coven was a bit boring." He pointed to a wand. "But there are plenty of options now."

There certainly were. An entire range of blue wands

stared back at me, from a deep, dark blue to a sapphire blue to a light eggshell blue.

"I should have brought Marley with me," I said. "She probably has an opinion."

"It's your wand," Wren said. "Why let your daughter choose for you?"

"Well, I figure it will be hers next year when she comes into her magic," I said.

Wren threw his head back and laughed. "Aren't you the optimistic one? What makes you think you'll have outgrown your starter wand in a year? That's true Rose confidence, that is."

My cheeks burned from embarrassment. I honestly hadn't considered that it might take years to master spells with a starter wand. So far, I'd managed to do magic with very little effort. I'd even managed to successfully use a fairy wand. Granted, it was in a time of stress, but still. It hadn't occurred to me that coven incantations would take years to learn.

"Sorry," I mumbled. "I didn't mean to come across as obnoxious. You're right. I'll choose a wand for me. It will be nice to let Marley choose her own next year. It'll be a cool little ritual."

Wren patted me on the back. "It will. A momentous occasion the two of you will long remember. I still remember when my parents took Dillon and me for our starter wands. They made such a fuss about it. Framed photographs. A celebratory dinner. You would have thought I'd earned my broomstick license."

"That must've been nice, though," I said. "Having big family events like that." I pictured all of the family events that must've taken place at Thornhold over the years, family gatherings that included my parents. I never had anything like that growing up or with Marley.

Starry Hollow presented us with the chance for a new chapter, one that involved rituals and traditions. It was nice.

"I keep getting drawn to that silver wand," I said, inclining my head toward it.

Wren lifted it from the shelf. "Nice one. It's got a little bit of sparkle in it. It'll match your cloak nicely."

He placed it in my hand and I felt the smooth shaft. When I placed my fingers on the end of the wand the way Linnea had shown me, Wren shot me a quizzical look.

"That's a pretty good grip you've got there already for a newbie," he said. "You must be a natural."

I remained silent. "So what happens now? Do I test it out?"

He nodded. "There's a room in the back."

I couldn't believe it. "A dressing room for wands?"

"You want to try on a cloak as well," he said.

"I'm getting a cloak, too?" Big day, indeed. It was like back-to-school shopping. Throw in a few number two pencils and I was education-ready.

"I should probably warn you that I'm supposed to report back to your aunt after we leave here," he said. "Let her know if we were successful."

I glanced up at him. "Why would you need to warn me about that?"

"Because if I tell her yes, then you'll probably be facing a celebratory dinner at Thornhold tonight." He gave me a wry smile. "It's a momentous occasion, remember?"

Got it. "Thanks for the heads up."

I followed Wren to the room at the back of the shop. We passed a gray-haired woman manning the counter. She had a round face that matched her body and kind eyes.

"Good day to you, Master-of-Incantation," she said, with a cheerful smile.

36

"Good day, Petunia," he said. "May I introduce Miss Ember Rose?"

The woman fixed her gaze on me, her eyes widening. "Not Yarrow?"

Wren's brow creased. "No, not Yarrow. Ember Rose."

"She knows my given name," I explained. Apparently, when I was born in Starry Hollow, I was given the name Yarrow, but my father changed it after he left town. Whether it was because he didn't like the name or to conceal my identity, I would never know.

Petunia examined me closely. "You are the perfect combination of your mother and father. Do you know that?"

"So I've been told," I said. "I've never seen a picture of my mother, though, so I'm not really sure how close the resemblance is." I shrugged. "I have to rely on what people have told me."

Petunia's face crumbled. "No one has shown you pictures of your mother?"

"No," I admitted. "Aunt Hyacinth apparently has photographs, but the family seems to think I should wait until she's in the right mood to ask to see them. I usually read people pretty well, but she's...tougher than most people."

Petunia slammed her hands down on the counter. "That's the most ridiculous thing I've ever heard. Those Roses are as daft as they are beautiful. I can help you resolve this issue right now, Ember."

Wren looked concerned. "Are you sure that's a good idea, Petunia? You don't want to risk incurring Hyacinth's wrath. Porter received a tongue lashing from her two years ago and he's still recovering."

The older woman blew a dismissive raspberry. "Hyacinth Rose-Muldoon only has as much power as we allow. Poor girl has never seen a picture of her own mother. Can you imagine such a thing? Wren, you and Dillon are very close to your parents. What would it be like to have never seen your mother's face? To have never heard her laugh? Gracious goddess, we owe Ember a piece of her past."

Wren's expression soured. "Come on then. Between a wand and a cloak, there suddenly seems to be a lot more to squeeze into the session and I'm on a schedule."

Petunia came out from behind the counter and accompanied us into the back room. She produced a wand from the inside pocket of her cloak. "I knew both of your parents, Yarrow."

"Ember," I corrected her.

"Yes, sorry. While I didn't know them as intimately as some, I'm certainly here as a resource for any questions you might have. And certainly for simple requests like pictures."

Petunia held out her wand and waved it at the far wall—it was a blank wall with no windows or artwork. She uttered an unintelligible phrase and an image appeared on the wall of a woman cradling a newborn baby. The woman's hair was long and dark like mine. The baby squirmed softly in her arms and she snuggled it to her breast. The woman glanced up, as though she felt herself being watched. A gasped escaped me as I stared into the face of my mother. Although I saw the resemblance immediately, it was fair to say that my mother's beauty far exceeded my own general attractiveness. It wasn't a particular feature—she wasn't striking like my Rose-Muldoon cousins—but there was something about the light reflected in her eyes. She radiated warmth and compassion. Emotions stirred within me as I watched the way she held the baby. Held *me*. I wondered what kind of person I would be now if she had raised me. Would I be more compassionate? Sweeter? More affectionate? I would never know. Sadly, another path had been chosen for me.

Petunia waved her wand again and another image

appeared. A younger version of my mother, smiling happily as she clutched a wand in her hand. A silver wand.

I glanced down at the starter wand in my hand and my chest ached.

"Okay," Wren said softly. "The wand might not be speaking to you out loud, but I never said anything about ignoring a blinking neon sign from the universe."

My fingers gripped the narrow starter wand. "You said they were all black, brown, and white back then."

"That was her mother's wand, passed down to her," Petunia said. "Your grandmother's. I remember it well. There was much discussion as to whether she should choose her own wand when her magic manifested. They came into the shop and Lily tried a few wands, but I could see her heart wasn't in it. She wanted her grandmother's."

"I don't suppose you know what happened to it," I said, my gaze still riveted to the image.

"I'm sorry, no," Petunia replied. "But the one in your hand is as close as you're going to get."

My index finger stroked the smooth wood. "I wonder who cleared out the cottage after my father left." Maybe it had been among her belongings. I'd have to ask Simon.

Petunia waved her wand and my breathing hitched. An image of my mother and father filled the wall. She wore a long, silver dress under her cloak and he wore a black cloak edged in silver braiding. Her dark hair hung in loose curls and she wore a headdress adorned with a silver moon. It was wonderful to see my father again. He'd always seemed like an older man to me, but here I could see evidence of his Rose heritage.

"Their wedding?" I asked. They looked very happy and very much in love.

The older witch nodded. "It was not the grand affair the

town hoped for, given your father's prominent position in the coven, but there were objections, you see."

"I know," I said. "I mean, I know my mother wasn't deemed worthy of marrying a Rose, but I don't know why."

"I wish I could say for certain," Petunia said. "I only know the rumors. That your aunt disapproved and she and your father argued over it. Then he married your mother anyway."

"Did they marry at Thornhold?" I asked.

"Gracious goddess, no," Petunia said. "Your aunt refused permission for that. Everyone was shocked when they moved into Rose Cottage. We were sure they'd have to live across town, away from your aunt."

"I'm surprised my father chose to live there," I said. "If he was being stubborn, he would have put as much distance between himself and his sister as possible."

"He did, eventually," Petunia said. "After all, the human world may as well be another planet."

"Some days, it seems that way," I agreed.

"I hate to cut you off," Wren said, "but I need to finish up our assignment. I've got a class to teach at the coven rec center."

"Sorry, Wren," I said. I couldn't tear my gaze away from the wall. Not while the image still hovered there.

"Stars and stones, don't be sorry," Wren said. "This is important. I realize that."

Petunia tucked away her wand and the image dissipated. A lump formed in my throat.

"You're welcome here anytime," Petunia said. "But your aunt will have access to far more than I do. You strike me as a woman of strong character. Don't be afraid to ask for what's yours. These memories are your birthright."

"Thank you so much, Petunia," I said. "You have no idea what this means to me."

She winked at me. "Judging from the tears in your eyes, I think I do." She left the room and closed the door behind her.

"Ready to try your starter wand?" Wren asked. "I'll give you five minutes."

I took a steadying breath and nodded. "Ready."

CHAPTER 5

THE ART GALLERY looked different in the light of day. All of the fancy trimmings were now absent and all remnants of the swanky event had been cleared away. I'd given Bentley the chance to complete the story on Trupti's show, but he quietly declined. He was still too hurt to return to the scene of his humiliation.

As annoying as Bentley could be, I found myself feeling sorry for him. His experience with Meadow was the downside of online dating. Here he thought he'd met the perfect partner, only to discover it was all a lie. In some ways, it must've been how Linnea felt when she discovered Wyatt's many infidelities. He wasn't the werewolf she thought she'd married. At least Bentley discovered Meadow's deceit before it got to a more serious point in the relationship.

Trupti stood at a table at the far side of the room, carefully wrapping a painting—I assumed in preparation for transport. She brightened when she saw me.

"Ember, what a nice surprise to see you again."

"Alec decided that I should finish the article that Bentley

42

started, so I thought it would be a good idea to follow up with you today on the results of the show."

Trupti inclined her head toward the package on the table. "This is the last one to go. I'm quite pleased with the results overall. I managed to sell half, which puts me in good stead."

"That's great," I said. I surveyed the walls of the art gallery, which still held the paintings I'd seen at the show with the giant pieces of fruit.

"It's a shame that the fruit paintings didn't sell, but I cannot say I'm surprised," she said, following my gaze. "It's almost as if people can sense the negativity behind them."

"Well, I've never had to interview anyone about an art show before, so I'm going to ask you questions and you're going to pretend I know what I'm doing."

She finished taping the last bit of brown paper and smiled. "I can see why Alec likes you."

"Excuse me? You must have me confused with someone else," I said, lying through my square human teeth. "He doesn't even want me to call him by his first name. I insisted on it. He still calls me Miss Rose."

She laughed lightly. "Yes, I noticed that. Very amusing. Alec can be…quite closed off if you do not put the effort in. You grow accustomed to it." She shrugged. "Or you don't. Either way, he will never change."

"I sort of have to get used to it," I said. "I work for him. If the worst thing that happens is he calls me Miss Rose for the rest of my career, it's not the end of the world."

Trupti finished wrapping the package and gave me a curious look. "You think it is only work to him? No, I don't suppose you will know him well enough to see the difference."

"How long have you known each other?"

She appeared thoughtful. "Fifty years, I think. Give or take."

I tried to disguise my shock. Trupti didn't look fifty years old, forget having known someone for fifty years. Paranormals had the lion's share of youth and beauty, that was for sure.

"Would you care for anything to drink?" she asked. "I'm suddenly very thirsty. Must be all the wine I've been drinking this week. It's been quite the celebration."

"Sure," I replied. "I had a hard time getting up the other morning. The whole cottage was tipped to the side. My daughter thought I was having some kind of brain embolism."

Trupti laughed. "I bet he likes that you have a daughter."

"Who?"

"Alec, of course. It was the main reason our relationship fell apart." She stared down at her ringless finger. "He wanted children, but I adamantly did not."

"Well, he couldn't have wanted them that badly. Otherwise, he'd have them by now."

"He's a vampire, Ember," she said. "He wants the whole package and he's prepared to wait for it. If he doesn't find the right woman in this century, he will simply wait for the next one."

Another century? That showed some hard-core patience.

She retrieved two glasses of water from the back room and handed one to me. By the time I'd taken a sip of mine, I noticed her glass was already empty. She wasn't kidding about being thirsty.

"So can I ask how much money you made from the show?" I asked.

Trupti's smile widened. "Right to the point, huh? I'm sure there were one hundred ways you could have tiptoed around that question and still received your answer."

"Yeah, but it would've taken an hour. I don't want to waste your time. I'm sure you're very busy with your...fruit."

"I won't give you the total figure," she said, "but the lowest-priced painting sold for ten thousand and the highest-priced painting sold for thirty."

My eyes popped. "For a picture? That you painted?" Consider my mind blown.

Trupti shrugged. "These are not unusual numbers, Ember. Not for me, anyway."

I whistled. "I'm in the wrong line of work." Then again, I'd always been in the wrong line of work. It was my career path —Jobs That Suck. Until now, anyway.

Trupti's dark eyes narrowed. "Ember," she said slowly. "Is it just me, or did the pear in that painting move?"

I craned my neck to see the painting of the giant pear on the wall. While I certainly didn't know the painting as well as she did, the image of the pear did seem slightly off-center now.

She flicked a dismissive finger. "I must be imagining things. Too much wine still in my system."

"What will you paint next?" I asked. "Is that how it works? The cycle starts all over again and you paint until your next show?"

Before she could answer, I heard the sound of tearing paper and whipped my head toward the source. The pear had not only moved—it had moved straight off the canvas. Now positioned in front of the painting was a giant pear. Unlike the one in the painting, this one had an angry face. A pear with slits for eyes and a mouthful of sharp teeth.

"Blood and apricots," Trupti said, her jaw dropping. "It's alive."

The sound of shredding alerted us to more escaped artwork. Giant pieces of fruit peeled off the canvases and landed on the floor with a collective thud. A scream pierced the air and I realized it had come from me. Every piece of painted fruit was now living and breathing on the gallery floor…eyeing us as a source of food.

"Hungry," the apple said, and chomped its teeth.

"We're not healthy," I cried, not thinking clearly. "*You* are healthy. You need to eat each other if you're hungry." Fruit cannibalism. Blech.

Trupti clasped my hand in hers. Her fear was palpable.

"This is my worst nightmare," she whispered.

I glanced back at the angry, hungry fruit. I mean, it was scary, but I wasn't sure it would be my worst nightmare.

"I'll text the sheriff," I said, and quickly sent off a message. It was hard to know what to say in order to be taken seriously, so I left the request for help as vague as possible.

The giant pieces of fruit hopped closer to us, enclosing us in a circle—we were in the middle of a fruit wrap. The only weapon I had was the empty glass in my hand. In one swift motion, I chucked the glass at the pear's head, piercing the skin. Juice dripped down the pear's side.

"Take that, pear," I said. "You're either too ripe or too soft. You're never just right."

Trupti gaped at me. "Ember, don't antagonize the fruit."

Too late. I turned my attention to the giant apple. "And you! Do you know how many times I choked on your skin? I'm surprised I'm still alive to tell the tale. My daughter makes me peel the skin off her apples." And I complained every single time, but no more.

The pear growled, angry about its pierced skin. I snatched the glass from Trupti's hand and threw it, this time at the approaching banana. The peel split and soft banana goo squished down the front of the banana's face.

The pieces of fruit advanced and Trupti dropped to her knees, caving under pressure. I glanced around the room, desperately seeking something else to use in self-defense. On the table was the pair of scissors Trupti had been using to cut the brown packaging paper. I didn't want to leave Trupti at her most vulnerable, but if I could get to the scissors, I could try to slice the fruit into manageable segments.

I crouched beside Trupti. "You stay here. I'm making a run for the scissors, but I won't leave you. I promise."

"No." She held my arm in a viselike grip. "You can't leave." Her fangs appeared, daring me to try.

Uh oh.

I needed the scissors. I focused my will and tried to use telekinesis to pull the scissors to me, but they only shifted less than an inch. I had to try something else. Something that allowed me to be in two places at once.

"Trupti, stay calm," I said. "I'm going to try something else."

I sat on the floor beside her and began to slow my breathing—easier said than done with raging fruit all around us. I relaxed my muscles and concentrated on separating my conscious self from my physical self. Finally I stood and looked down at my body to make sure I'd succeeded. Trupti hadn't noticed. She was too overcome with anxiety.

My astral self dashed between the banana and the apple and I heard the snap of their teeth as I moved past them. I reached for the scissors and prayed I'd be able to handle them. Marigold said I'd be able to manipulate physical objects, but we hadn't actually gotten to that part yet.

I spun back toward the fruit and snapped the scissors in half so that I had a blade in each hand. At least they were industrial scissors. If I could take their attention away from Trupti, then she might regain her composure and be helpful. She was of no use to me huddled on the floor.

All right, banana, I said in my head. *Time to split.* I cringed at my own mom joke since Marley wasn't here to do it for me. It was probably for the best that my astral self couldn't speak.

I sliced through the banana's middle and it toppled over. The apple tried to bite me, but its teeth met with empty air. I jammed the tip of the blade into its side and twisted. Its scream was more high-pitched than I anticipated.

I hastened a glance at Trupti, who was staring gobsmacked at my slumped form on the floor beside her. I continued my attack, stabbing and slicing the fruit until they were nothing but small, squishy pieces on the floor. I felt a strong tug at the base of my spine and realized it was my body pulling me back. I'd spent too much time outside of it and it wanted me back. I walked over to my physical form and set the blades next to me before rejoining my body.

"That was incredible," Trupti said, her voice trembling. "Truly. In all my years, I have never seen anything quite like it. For a vampire, that is saying something."

My heart was racing and I gave myself a moment to recover. "I'm glad it worked. I was worried."

"I'm sorry I couldn't be more help to you," she said.

The door to the gallery burst open, signaling the arrival of Sheriff Nash. He barely made it through the door when he saw the mess on the floor.

"It looks like a massacre in here," he said. "What happened?"

Trupti hugged herself, still trying to calm her nerves. She told the story to the best of her ability, stopping for deep, cleansing breaths on occasion. She made me sound like a bona fide fruit ninja.

"You really did all that?" Sheriff Nash asked, glancing around the floor at the fruit remnants.

"Death by fruit wasn't really an option," I said. "The adrenaline kicked in."

"Looks that way," the sheriff said. "Any idea who may have done this to you?"

"It was Ashara," Trupti said. "I know it."

MAGIC & MISCHIEF

"Who's Ashara?" I asked.

"Another artist," the sheriff said. "Why do you think so? Are you two in an argument?"

"Not openly," Trupti admitted. "She's always been jealous of my career. And she didn't attend my event."

"Did she give a reason?" I asked.

Trupti huffed. "She claimed she had to practice for her own performance, but it's probably because she was planning this attack and felt too guilty to look me in the eye. She even sent me a fruit basket as an apology gift. If that's not evidence, I don't know what is."

The sheriff and I exchanged uncertain glances. It didn't seem plausible to me, but I had no idea who Ashara was. Maybe these artist types were all nuts.

"Where's the fruit basket now?" the sheriff asked.

"I threw it away," Trupti said. "It was insulting."

"Okay, listen. I'm going to need to call in my crew to comb the gallery for evidence," the sheriff said. "Unfortunately, that means leaving everything in its current state for now. Can you handle that?"

She nodded. "I'll go home and sleep, if that's okay with you."

"Do whatever you need to do," he said, placing a supportive hand on her shoulder. "Let me get you a glass of water."

"The door is over there," Trupti said, pointing. "There's a kitchenette."

I stayed with Trupti while the sheriff disappeared. I noticed that he made a few observations on his way to the back room. The drink was a nice touch, but I suspected it was more of an excuse to get the lay of the land. He returned quickly with a full glass of water, which Trupti gulped down greedily.

"Fear can make you thirsty," the sheriff said.

"Like you would know," Trupti said, handing him the empty glass. "You're a werewolf and the sheriff. I highly doubt you've had much experience with fear."

His expression darkened. "We all have our fears, Trupti. And yours is nothing to be embarrassed about. Our fears are often irrational."

"That's definitely true," I said. "I used to be afraid of falling into sidewalk grates. I would walk around them no matter how crowded the sidewalk was. I took a lot of elbows to the ribs thanks to that particular fear."

The sheriff frowned. "Okay, maybe that one you should be embarrassed about."

"Hey," I objected.

The sheriff turned his attention back to Trupti. "Is there someone you can call to escort you home?"

"I can do it." Alec appeared seemingly out of thin air.

"How did you know?" I asked, incredulous. Exactly how far did his telepathy reach? Could he listen to me when I was home alone in bed? I shivered at the thought.

"I texted him," Trupti said.

Phew. My body relaxed.

"Trupti, what happened?" Alec asked. He noticed the empty canvasses on the wall behind us. "Did you have another breakdown?"

Trupti's dark eyes clouded over. "No breakdown, Alec. This was real and spectacularly awful. Ask Ember."

I gestured to the remains of the fruit on the floor around us. "It was the Day of the Living Fruit around here for a good twenty minutes."

"They had teeth," Trupti blurted, and tears streaked her cheeks.

Alec placed a protective arm around her. "It's all over now," he said in a soothing tone. "Let me drive you home."

"Thank you," Trupti said softly, and leaned against his solid frame.

I watched as they left the gallery together. I'd never seen Alec in compassionate mode before. It suited him.

"They used to date, you know," the sheriff said.

"I know," I said.

He cocked an eyebrow, examining me. "They seem cozy now."

"He's being a good friend," I said. "I expect nothing less from a gentleman like Alec."

Sheriff Nash began poking through the debris, careful to keep his boots clean. "You really think he's a gentleman?"

"I've seen nothing to suggest otherwise," I replied. "He treats everyone with polite deference."

"Polite deference?" he repeated with a slow grin. "Rose, you've got to stop thumbing through your thesaurus at night. Get a hobby. Or maybe a boyfriend."

"It's not me," I said. "It's Marley. Her vocabulary rubs off on me."

"Oh, sure. Blame the child."

I folded my arms and studied him. "Why do I get the sense that you expect me to be jealous of Alec and Trupti?"

He gave me a look of mock innocence. "Me? I didn't say that."

"You implied it."

He shook his head. "Nope. Must be your imagination. The one that thinks sidewalk grates are a menace."

I shook a finger at him. "You'd better watch it, Sheriff."

His mouth quirked. "Or what? You'll use your fruit ninja skills against me?"

I moved to punch his arm just as the door opened, and the forensics team poured into the gallery. I pulled back at the last second. As much as the sheriff frustrated me, I didn't want to disrespect him in front of his subordinates. I wasn't sure why exactly. It never would've stopped me before.

"Time to get to work, Rose," the sheriff said. "Look at the bright side. I guess you'll have a new byline. Be careful. Bentley will start to resent you."

"Bentley resented me the minute I stepped through the door."

Sheriff Nash laughed. "Probably even before that."

I didn't argue. "I'm going home to shower."

The sheriff pretended to hold his nose. "Good idea."

I glared at him. "You're very mature. You know that?"

He tapped the star pinned to his shirt. "Still the sheriff."

I shook my head. "I don't know what this town was thinking."

"Lighten up, Rose. You're just upset because your boyfriend left with another woman."

My eyes bulged and I balled my fists. "He is *not* my boyfriend."

Sheriff Nash laughed and pointed at my face. "Do you know your eyes actually look more blue when you're angry? How is that possible?"

I gave him a hard shove before stomping out of the gallery. He was lucky I had to leave the scissors behind as evidence or there may have been an 'accident' on my way out.

I hated to admit it, but I was finally beginning to understand my aunt's attitude toward werewolves.

CHAPTER 6

MARLEY WAS on the edge of her seat as I shared the story of my art gallery adventure over dinner.

"I can't believe it," she said, her blue eyes shining. "I wish you had a video of it. Imagine the hits on YouTube."

"I think it would frighten kids away from fruit for the rest of their lives. Parents would be outraged."

"It sounds like the pear was the worst," Marley said.

"That's because Trupti hated pears the most."

"What a weird hex," Marley said. "Do you think the fruit would have been able to kill her if you hadn't been there?"

"Probably not," I said, although I wasn't confident. "Teeth on fruit are downright scary, though."

Marley pushed her peas around her plate. "Aren't peas technically a fruit?"

"No peas were harmed in the making of today's nightmare," I said in my best television voice.

"I'll never look at apples the same way again," Marley said.

"You and me both."

"So why would someone bring Trupti's artwork to life?" Marley asked.

I scraped the last of my dinner off my plate. "She's convinced it was a rival artist. Someone who wanted to frighten Trupti by confronting her with her worst fear. I'm going to pay the woman a visit tomorrow and see what I can learn."

Marley sat in thoughtful silence for a moment. "If someone did that to you, what do you think would happen?"

"I'd fall down a sidewalk grate, naturally."

Marley laughed. "Really? That can't be your answer."

I cupped her chin with my hand. "You don't want to know my answer." Not only because she was an anxious child, but also because my worst fear had nearly come true when Jimmy the Lighter showed up at our apartment to murder us. Losing Karl and my father was bad enough. Losing Marley was unfathomable.

Marley nibbled a piece of chicken. "I think mine would be stupidity." She paused. "Or maybe falling from a great height. Or drowning." She swallowed a gulp of chocolate milk. "Or a ghost taking over my body and pretending to be me."

I eyed her curiously. "That last one is very specific."

"I saw it on a television show once."

"With Miss Kowalski?"

She nodded. "I promised I wouldn't tell you that she let me watch it. I begged her."

"Doesn't matter. She should've known better."

Marley shrugged. "Nothing you can do about it now."

PP3's ears perked up, followed by a knock on the door.

"No barking," I said. "Must be a friendly." I left the table and peeked out the window. "It's Simon."

Marley ran to join me as I opened the door.

"Hi, Simon," Marley said.

"Miss Marley," he said with a bow. "Miss Ember. My lady requests your presence in the main house in thirty minutes."

"Both of us?" I queried.

"Both of you," he said.

"Is this about my wand and cloak?" I asked.

Marley's head swiveled toward me. "You got your wand and cloak? Why didn't you tell me?"

"I've been waiting to show you when I had time," I said. "I thought it would be a fun surprise."

Marley folded her arms and glared at me. "We're not supposed to keep secrets from each other. That's your rule, remember?"

"It wasn't a secret," I insisted. "It was going to be a surprise."

"Shall I inform my lady that you'll attend?" Simon asked, unperturbed by our squabbling.

"Yes, we'll be there," I said.

"A bit of advice, Miss Ember," Simon said. "Bring the wand and wear the cloak."

"Yes, sir." I saluted him before closing the door.

"Should we eat dessert before we go?" Marley asked.

"You're a crafty one," I said. "You know perfectly well Aunt Hyacinth will serve sweets."

She gave me a sly smile. "I don't know what you mean, Mom."

"We don't have time for double desserts. Finish your dinner and then we'll need to make ourselves presentable."

"Good point," Marley said. "Your hair looks like it got trapped in the ceiling fan paddles again."

"Hey," I objected. "I can't help when it's windy."

"You can help what you do about it when you're indoors," Marley pointed out.

I touched my hair and felt the tangle of knots. "Okay, you win. I'll brush my hair. I don't need Aunt Hyacinth staring down her nose at me."

"She'll do that anyway," Marley said.

"You're probably right."

Marley was right. Half an hour later, I stood in front of Aunt Hyacinth in my silver cloak as she stared down her nose at me. She wore one of her usual kaftans—this one was a cheerful green color with a picture of an enormous white cat head on the back. If this look ever caught on within the coven, I'd be guaranteed a life of celibacy.

My aunt's gaze was drawn to the wand clutched in my hand. "Interesting choice," she murmured. "May I?"

I handed the wand to her. She studied it closely, like she was searching for hidden markings in the wood.

"It's good craftsmanship," she said, and handed it back to me. "Whatever persuaded you to choose silver?"

"We're the Silver Moon coven," I said. "My cloak is silver. It seemed fitting."

"Indeed." Aunt Hyacinth scrutinized the robe. "We'll need to let the hem out a bit. You're taller than the average witch."

"Not as tall as your kids," I said.

"No." She wore a proud smile. "My children are exceptionally tall. The perfect height. Above average yet not so tall that they seem abnormal."

"There's nothing normal about them," I said.

Aunt Hyacinth leveled a gaze at me. "I beg your pardon?"

"I mean they're like superheroes," I said. "Each one is more powerful and more gorgeous than the last one. It's unfair to the rest of the coven."

"Yes, I've often heard that. Nothing to be done about it, I'm afraid. Some gene pools are worth swimming in."

Ew. "Um, I guess."

"Marley, would you like a Wish cookie?" Aunt Hyacinth asked. "Simon has a tray of them in the kitchen."

"You definitely want one," I told Marley. I'd had one at my first coven meeting and it was nothing short of amazing.

Marley's eyes lit up. "I'm on it."

"She's very much like you," Aunt Hyacinth remarked, once Marley was out of earshot.

"Not really," I said. "I think all the good genes skipped a generation."

"Don't sell yourself short, darling," my aunt said. "You have much to offer. While we're on the subject, how was your session with Wren?"

"Good."

She eyed me suspiciously. "That's oddly brief for someone with your…verbal skills."

"Is that your polite way of calling me a big mouth?"

Aunt Hyacinth suppressed a smile. "I would never say anything so offensive."

"I'd like to see pictures of my parents," I blurted. *There you go, Aunt Hyacinth. Verbal skills in action.*

She lifted one blond, sculpted eyebrow. "Pictures?"

"You must have a few packed away somewhere," I said. "Or maybe you can magic up a few."

"Magic up?"

"It's a verb," I insisted.

She clasped her hands in front of her. "What's made you so eager to see them?"

I opened my mouth and closed it again. Was that seriously a question that needed an answer?

I tapped my chin, pretending to think. "Let's see. What's made me so eager? Well, my mother died when I was a baby. I have no memory of her, although everyone says I look like her. My father acted like his life began in New Jersey with me. The only times I ever saw him happy were the times *I* made him happy. Do you know how much pressure that is on a child? To be a father's only source of happiness?"

I noticed the muscle in Aunt Hyacinth's cheek twitch. "Do you think Marley feels the same as you?"

I blinked. "About my father?"

"About you, darling. You've resigned yourself to a lifetime of devotion to your daughter. Don't you realize you're putting the same pressure on her that you believe your father put on you?"

I stood rooted in place. I'd never considered the hypocrisy of my actions. I'd always believed I was being self-less, sacrificing my happiness for hers—no doubt the same belief my father held.

"I just want to put her first," I said. "I get such a short time with her before she grows up…"

Aunt Hyacinth remained silent, letting the realization sink in.

Oh. "It isn't the same," I insisted.

Aunt Hyacinth patted my arm. "Of course not. Would you like a cocktail? I'll have Simon bring two fizzlewick martinis."

"Sure. Why not? I could use a drink after the weird day I had."

She inclined her head. "So the rumors are true? About the artwork?"

"You're seriously plugged in around here, aren't you?"

Aunt Hyacinth offered a vague smile. "I'm on the Council of Elders, my dear. We're like the all-seeing eye of Starry Hollow."

"That's…creepy."

She rang a silver bell and Simon appeared with two cock-tails on a tray. He handed one to each of us.

"Thank you, Simon," my aunt said. "How is Marley getting on with her cookie?"

"Enjoying it immensely, my lady."

"Excellent." She sipped her drink. "That will be all for now."

"As you wish." Simon bowed and left the room.

"I heard you employed an interesting skill to defend yourself against the...vengeful fruit."

"I used astral projection like Marigold taught me."

"And you were able to control a pair of scissors in your apparitional form."

I nodded. "I wasn't sure if it would work, but it did."

"That's impressive, Ember. You realize that, don't you?"

I laughed. "*I* was impressed. That's for sure."

"Wren says you're a natural with a wand, too."

"He's jumping the gun," I said. "I only held the starter wand. I didn't get to do much with it yet."

Her gaze flickered over me. "Be that as it may, I'm pleased with your progress so far."

"Speaking of progress, how's Florian doing with his volunteer work?" I'd been so wrapped up in my own life, I had no idea whether Florian was keeping up his end of the bargain.

"Like you, he's decided to work with the tourism board."

Ruh roh. Poor Aster. She took her role there very seriously.

"That's great. I'm glad he's making an effort." I took a huge gulp of the martini.

"I think you've inspired him, Ember. He sees how you've worked hard and quickly become a member of the community. He wants that for himself."

That was wishful thinking. "I think it's more likely the offer of a new boat that's inspired him."

She pressed her lips together. "Perhaps."

"So when can I see pictures of my parents?" Persistence was my middle name, or should have been.

My aunt smiled demurely over the rim of her cocktail glass. "All in good time, Ember. All in good time."

I found Ashara practicing in the performing arts arena. The venue was like a small stadium, open air with bleacher-style seating. It didn't take long to see why she needed to practice in a place like this. From the back of the arena, I saw flames shoot high into the sky. Ashara stood on the stage, waiting for the ball of fire to return to her. I watched in awe as she opened her mouth wide and swallowed the flame whole.

Great balls of fire—literally. My feet were cemented in place. Her act was absolutely mesmerizing. She produced another ball of fire in her hand and began to juggle, creating two more fireballs to keep in the air. Ashara's 'art' was nothing like fruit paintings. This woman was a true performance artist.

After a few more minutes, she noticed my presence. No doubt her routine required her full concentration.

"The arena is closed now," she said. "I am here only for a practice session."

I took a few hesitant steps toward her. "I'm not here to see the show," I said. Although now that I'd had a sneak peek, I was inclined to buy tickets. I'd even bring Marley with me. She'd be enthralled.

Ashara inclined her head. "Why are you here?"

"I came to talk to you about Trupti."

Her expression remained blank. "What about her? Did something happen at her exhibition? I was sorry I could not attend, but I had an engagement of my own."

"The show was good," I said. "I was there. I understand you sent a gift the next day."

Ashara nodded. "That's right. I sent her a fruit basket.

Under the circumstances, I thought it was appropriate. I wanted to apologize for missing the show."

"You know her paintings of fruit are an expression of trauma," I said.

Ashara chuckled lightly. "To be honest, I have never truly understood Trupti's art. Just as she does not understand mine." With that statement, Ashara burst into flames and I gasped. The woman literally set herself on fire with her own body.

She burned brightly for a moment, before the flames dissolved. Ashara stood on the stage, still fully clothed.

"How did you do that?" I asked, stunned. "Are you a witch that controls fire?"

If I could control rain or wind, then it seemed likely that some witches could control fire.

"I'm a phoenix shifter," Ashara said. "My very essence is fire. It is not so much that I control the flames as they are part of me."

"What else can you do?" I moved slightly closer to the stage, but not so close that errant flames would singe my eyebrows.

"I am just about to practice my finale," Ashara said. "Stay and you will see."

I sat at the end of the nearest bleacher, mesmerized. Ashara brought her arms to her sides and closed her eyes. Her body began to glow yellow, then orange, then a deep sunset until she burned red from the inside out. Wings sprouted from her back, large and flamed. Her human body morphed into what could only be described as a firebird. She shot into the air like a firework and exploded into a million particles. It was the ultimate light show. As the pieces drifted back to the ground, they turned to black ash. One by one, they continued to fall until they formed a black pile of debris on the stage. When the last piece fell, the black ash began to take a human shape, rising from the stage floor. Finally I could make out Ashara's outline. The black ash turned to black skin and hair. My jaw hung open as I watched Ashara reform in front of me. She bowed and I clapped heartily.

"Great popcorn balls of fire," I said. "That has to be the most incredible thing I've seen in Starry Hollow."

Ashara smiled broadly. "Thank you very much. I have been preparing for weeks."

"I have to be honest. Trupti has this idea that the two of you are competitive, but your art is nothing alike. Why would she think that?"

Ashara crossed the stage and came to sit beside me on the bench.

"Trupti and I have a long history of competition in the art world. We were both in the market for patrons at the same time. My act was different then, less showy. I had not truly embraced my inner phoenix at that point."

"So Trupti gained more patrons," I said.

She nodded. "To be fair, her artwork was more interesting then. We seem to have swapped roles over time. I feel that her art has gone stale, while mine has evolved."

"She thinks you put a curse on the fruit basket that you sent because you were jealous of her show," I said.

Ashara's brow furrowed. "What kind of curse?"

"All the fruit from her paintings came to life and attacked us."

To her credit, Ashara didn't laugh. In fact, her expression turned grim.

"That must've been very upsetting for her."

"She was barely functional. I didn't know a vampire could be traumatized like that."

"Our art is essentially an extension of ourselves. It must've felt deeply troubling. Self-hatred run amok."

"I'm just glad I was there to help," I said. "If she'd been alone, I don't know what might've happened."

Ashara pressed her lips together. "Best not to dwell on such things. I will send her a gift to let her know I'm sorry and that I'm thinking of her."

I cast a sidelong glance at her. "As long as it isn't a fruit basket."

Ashara managed a small smile. "Indeed."

CHAPTER 7

AFTER MY VISIT TO ASHARA, I went to the office to give my article on Trupti's show a final polish. Part of me wanted to ask Bentley to read it and give it his blessing before I turned it in to Alec, but I was too pigheaded to ask for help. Knowing Bentley, he'd mark it up with a red pen just to be a jerk.

When I arrived at my desk, Bentley was hunched over his keyboard, typing with unusual slowness.

"What's wrong, buttercup?" I asked. "Still upset about your girlfriend?"

"She's definitely *not* my girlfriend," he said.

"Are you messaging her right now?"

"No, I'm working," he said sullenly. "I blocked her on MagicMirror, so she can't message me."

Ouch. "That seems harsh. Are you sure you want to do that?"

"She lied to me," Bentley said. He seemed so unlike himself—so defeated.

"But the two of you have been messaging for a while," I said. "Don't you feel like you got to know the real Meadow?"

He gave an adamant shake of his head. "She was an illusion. A fantasy. There is no real Meadow."

At that moment, the front door swung open and a pretty young woman stepped inside. She had large brown eyes and smooth, bronzed skin. Her brown hair was pulled back in a ponytail and I immediately recognized the silver scarf tied at her throat. Evidently, so did Bentley.

"Meadow?" he croaked.

She followed the sound of his voice. "Bentley?"

He pushed back his chair, thoroughly confused. "But...I don't understand."

She blinked. "You told me where you work. I'm sorry. I don't mean to seem like a stalker."

"I know, but..."

"Listen, I'm sorry I didn't show up at the gallery," Meadow said, taking a hesitant step forward. "I lost my nerve. Please don't block my messages."

"You didn't show up?" Bentley repeated. "But you did. You were there."

Meadow scrunched her perfect nose. "No, I wasn't. I got cold feet." Her gaze dropped to the floor. "I've enjoyed talking to you so much that I worried you wouldn't like me in person."

Bentley covered his mouth with his hands, trying to come to grips with what happened at the art gallery.

"Can you confirm that you're not a yeti?" I asked.

Meadow faced me. "A yeti? No, of course not. I'm a nymph. Bentley knows that."

Bentley closed his eyes and drew a deep breath. "I was so worried that you wouldn't be as wonderful as you seemed."

"Bentley," I said. "Do you know what this means? That yeti was your nightmare come to life." It all made sense now.

"But why would someone curse me?" Bentley asked. "I know Trupti blamed Ashara..."

"It wasn't Ashara, and I don't know why you were targeted." Not yet anyway.

"Will you ever forgive me?" Meadow asked.

Bentley closed the gap between them. "Of course I will. Would you like to go for a coffee now so we can talk?"

Meadow broke into a huge smile. "I would love that. Are you sure?"

"Definitely." Bentley turned toward me. "You don't mind, do you?"

"Why would I mind?"

"You'll be the only one here," Bentley replied.

I glanced around the office. "Tanya will be back soon." Not that it mattered. Why would I object to being alone in the office? It wasn't like it was a haunted house.

Bentley and Meadow were still gazing at each other when they left. I had to admit that I felt a brief pang of envy. I didn't mind that it was just Marley and me—I wouldn't trade her for anything or anyone in the world—but there were moments when I longed for the companionship. The spark of hope. Not that I would confess that to anyone. The heartbreak of losing Karl was enough for one lifetime. I didn't want to go through that kind of loss again, even a breakup would be too much for me to handle. And Marley was older now. She'd remember more. I couldn't hide in the closet and cry like I used to, with PP3 whining outside the door. The only safe place was the shower, where I could rinse away my tears before drying off and facing the day.

I busied myself with finishing the article about Trupti's show. I'd need to ask Alec how he wanted to handle the strange nightmare curse that was plaguing residents. I bet Milo Jarvis was a victim, too. That would explain his nude public speaking at the board meeting.

What was the commonality among the victims? I couldn't think of any link between Trupti and Bentley except for

Alec. Was it revenge against Alec for something? Then why not curse him directly? And it wasn't like Alec particularly loved Bentley. They had an employer/fanboy relationship at best. There was always a chance that one of them had been cursed by accident. Maybe the spell caster had missed his intended target. Of course, that didn't take Milo into account.

I tried to focus on my notes from the art gallery. I wrote about the inspiration for Trupti's paintings and tried to describe the art without sounding like a complete moron. I didn't know how to talk about art. I sighed. I'd need to ask Bentley for help after all. Of course, he'd likely insist on getting credit…

"Miss Rose."

I jumped. "Alec, how do you do that?"

"My brain sends a message to my mouth…"

"Hardy har." I glared at him. "And here I was talking about your polite deference."

His green eyes glimmered. "Is that so? And with whom were you engaged in such riveting conversation?"

"Sheriff Nash."

His smile faded. He plucked a bottle of water from Bentley's desk. "Forgive me. I am rather parched."

The vampire made drinking a glass of water look like a sensual experience. Just watching the way his lips touched the rim of the bottle's lip made my body tingle. When he set the bottle down and looked at me, I quickly glanced away.

"Shields are up," I whispered to myself. I pictured my thoughts wrapped in the black cloak the way Aster and Sterling had taught me. A huge black cloak with Velcro. And thick, braided rope.

Alec's mouth quirked. "Struggling with something?"

My eyes widened. "Who, me? Nope. No struggles here. How was your water? Delicious, right?"

"It hit the spot." He paused. "That is the human expression, is it not?"

"It is," I said. "So would you like to read what I've written so far about Trupti's show? I thought it was best to leave out the part about the paintings attacking us. No one would ever want to buy from her again."

"Very wise, Miss Rose. She is a dear friend of mine. I would not wish to do her career any harm."

"Me neither." I noticed a gradual shift in his expression. Why was he looking at me like that? "Alec, is everything okay?"

He blinked. "Of course it is. Why wouldn't it be?"

"I don't know," I said. "You had a funny expression on your face. Like I was Tweety Bird and you were Sylvester."

He cocked his head. "I have no earthly idea what that means."

The door opened behind us and a woman stepped into the office wearing a red dress. It reminded me of the one I wore to Trupti's show. The woman looked mildly confused.

"Can I help you with something?" I asked.

She didn't have the chance to respond. Alec lunged forward, fangs exposed, and pounced on the woman. I watched in horror as he grabbed her around the waist and tilted her head to the side, presenting him with a bare neck. Sweet baby Elvis. What was he about to do?

His head reared back and I screamed, "Alec, no!"

It was too late. His fangs sank into her vulnerable skin. Oddly, she made no sound. She simply sank into the bite the way you would into a kiss. A soft moan escaped her lips and he bit down harder. Blood trickled down her neck and into the cleavage of her dress.

My heart pounded. "Alec, what are you doing? You're hurting her."

He ignored me, lost in bloodlust. His grip on her grew

tighter and his fangs sank deeper. I didn't know what to do. I wanted to help this woman, but I also wanted to help myself escape before he turned his fangs on me.

I glanced around the room, trying to figure out the best way to deal with the situation. I wasn't even sure what the real defenses against vampires were. Not that I had any garlic on hand, but would that even work? I had to learn things, not just for my sake but also for Marley's.

I surveyed the room for anything that might help. I certainly didn't have access to any crosses. I pulled out my phone and searched for an image. It was the best I could do. When I found a good one, I held up the phone in front of Alec's face. He stopped sucking his victim's blood long enough to glance at the screen.

"Why are you showing me a picture of a pagan cross?"

I looked quickly at the screen. "It has to be a particular kind of cross?" Although this one looked fancy, I figured a cross was a cross.

"You're right," he said. "It doesn't matter because crosses don't do anything to vampires. That's simply a myth."

I fervently began to Google protections against vampires. I didn't really have time to figure out how to separate the wheat from the chaff.

"If you go to the website by Dr. Byron Von Clamps," he said, "he has some excellent information about vampires."

When he returned his focus to his victim, I pretended to type in Dr. Van Clamp's name. Instead, I shot off an S.O.S. text to Sheriff Nash. He was probably kicking himself for giving me his number. It seemed so long ago that we'd gone to the high school to check Yuri's locker.

The text was marked as sent. Now I just had to stay alive until he arrived. Watching the way Alec was devouring this poor woman, I wasn't sure whether five minutes would be long enough. Maybe if I could distract him for a few minutes…

"Alec," I said, unfastening the top button of my shirt. "Would you mind telling me what my blood type is? I think they told me in the hospital that I was B positive, but that was ten years ago. My memory is a bit fuzzy." I angled my head to give him an excellent view of my neck. Not that I wanted him to bite me. I only wanted to draw his attention away from the woman he was currently in the process of murdering.

He kept a firm grip on the woman as he glanced at me. "Miss Rose, if you would please be so kind as to button your shirt." He said each word slowly and deliberately.

I remained in the same position. "What's the matter? My blood isn't good enough for you? I'm a little insulted." The sound of my heartbeat thudded in my ears as I waited to see what he would do. I hoped Sheriff Nash came on four furry feet instead of two booted ones. Four would be faster.

Alec's nostrils flared. "Miss Rose, I will not ask again. Cover your neck or, I promise, you will regret it."

I flipped my dark hair over my shoulder and pulled the shirt further down, exposing even more skin. At least if he was talking to me, then he wasn't biting her.

He pushed the woman aside and stalked toward me.

The front door opened and Sheriff Nash appeared in the doorway. He didn't hesitate to act. He drew his gun and fired at Alec's back.

"No!" I said. What was he doing?

Alec dropped to the floor in front of me and Sheriff Nash hurried to restrain him.

"You shot him, dingbat," I yelled. "Are the handcuffs really necessary?"

"Don't worry," he said. "I didn't use a bullet. I used a tranquilzer. We have special ones we keep in stock for this kind of incident."

What kind of incident was that exactly? A rogue vampire attack?

I studied Alec's limp body on the floor and felt a pang of guilt.

"What about help for the woman?" I asked.

The sheriff gave me a quizzical look. "What woman?"

I peered over the men to where the woman in the red dress had been, but there was no one there. My brow furrowed.

"I don't understand," I said. "He was attacking a woman in a red dress."

The sheriff surveyed the room. "Well, there's no one here now."

"She was bleeding," I said. "He was going to kill her." I ran over to where she'd been standing to look for traces of blood. The floor was clean. My head began to swim. "I don't understand." I needed to go look for her. If she was wandering the streets alone, she was injured and needed help.

Sheriff Nash examined me. "Rose, I would have seen someone leaving as I was coming in, don't you think? I certainly would've noticed a bleeding woman in a red dress. Hard to miss, even for an incompetent sheriff like me."

I sat in the nearest chair and tried to make sense of what had just happened.

"I'll take Alec down to the station and sequester him until he cools off." He eyed me curiously. "What did you do to set him off?"

"What did I do?" I asked indignantly. "That's victim blaming at its finest."

His expression softened. "I didn't mean it like that. It's just that Alec is so tightly wound. I thought you must've done something to really provoke him. Knowing you, that was not out of the realm."

I watched in awe as Sheriff Nash lifted the vampire right over his shoulder like he weighed nothing.

"Wow," I said. "I didn't know werewolves were that strong."

He winked at me. "Not all of them are. Why don't you come with me down to the station and we can talk about what happened?"

I nodded, my nerves still shot. "On one condition."

"What's that?"

"Do you keep any alcohol there?"

He grinned. "I might know of a secret stash. Come on."

CHAPTER 8

I SAT WRAPPED in a blanket in the sheriff's office awaiting his return. He and Deputy Bolan had placed Alec in a secure room downstairs, specially designed for vampire containment. I felt horrible for Alec. It was so undignified. He'd be mortified when he snapped out of whatever weird state he was in.

Sheriff Nash swaggered into the office and closed the door behind him. "Ready for that drink?"

I nodded. "What kind of magical ale do you keep in here?"

"It's called bourbon," he replied.

"Bourbon?" I echoed. "That's what we drink in the human world."

He set a bottle on the desk. "And it's good enough for me." He retrieved two shot glasses from the top drawer and filled each one to the brim. When he finished, he handed one to me.

"Bottoms up, Rose." He tipped back his glass and drained it in the blink of an eye.

I quickly followed suit. The alcohol burned my throat, but I didn't care. I needed to blur the memory of what I'd witnessed. It was too unsettling. That wasn't the Alec Hale I knew. The vampire I'd seen was unhinged and dangerous, not the vampire of expensive suits and epic fantasy novels.

"Guess you've never seen a vamp act out before," the sheriff said.

"Um, no. Can't say that I have." I swallowed hard. "Does this happen often?"

The sheriff shook his head. "Not here in Starry Hollow. Vamps here are more civilized."

"Alec wasn't himself."

"Well, he was, just not the way you're used to seeing him."

"He was like a...a..."

"A monster?" Sheriff Nash finished for me.

I hated to use the word monster. I was very fond of Alec. "Yes," I whispered.

"There's a monster lurking in most men," the sheriff said. "If you're lucky, you'll never meet it."

"That's cynical of you," I said. "What about you?"

He tapped his chest. "I've got the wolf."

"Wolves aren't monsters."

"Can be. Anything can be under the right circumstances." He poured himself another drink and I realized how hard his expression had become. Not the usual lopsided grin I'd grown accustomed to.

"You normally reject alcohol when you're on duty," I pointed out.

"Special circumstances," he said. "Plus, I was thirsty."

"Alcohol dries you out," I said. "It doesn't hydrate you."

"A minor detail." He polished off the bourbon. "More for you?"

I held up a hand. "I'm good." As much as I wanted another one, I had to be coherent to take care of Marley after school. Responsible Parenting 101.

"Did he try to bite you?" Sheriff Nash asked.

"No," I said, trying to block the memory of the woman from my mind. "He was resisting the urge. He definitely wanted to, though."

"No kidding. He's probably been resisting the urge to bite you since the moment he met you."

"He's never acted like this before," I said. "I mean, I feel like I can always see his fangs, so I'm constantly reminded he's a vampire..."

Sheriff Nash sighed. "You still haven't figured that one out, have you?"

My brow creased. "Figured what out?"

"For a smartass, you're not always so smart."

I crossed my arms. "Feeling brave now that you've tossed back a couple, Sheriff?"

"In my experience, you see a vampire's fangs for three reasons. One is they're hungry. Two is they're pissed off. Three is they're very turned on." He waited for me to catch up.

"So his fangs are like..." I groped for appropriate words. "A vampire erection?" Okay, I landed somewhere west of appropriate words.

Sheriff Nash chuckled. "You hit the nail on the head." We groaned simultaneously. "Stars and stones. No more lewd comments from either of us." His eyes suddenly flashed a bright yellow and a guttural noise escaped his lips.

"Sheriff?" I leaned forward to inspect his face.

"No," he said in a hoarse whisper. "Not now." His body twisted and he howled in pain.

I leaped to my feet, nearly knocking over the chair in the process. "Sheriff, what's wrong?"

His features began to change before my eyes. His skin stretched and his hair grew. He forced himself to meet my horrified gaze.

"Rose, run." His voice was nearly a growl.

I sprinted from the room and slammed the door behind me. "Deputy! Deputy, I need you." I saw no sign of Deputy Bolan or anyone else for that matter. Where did everyone go?

The office door burst open and a large gray wolf stepped across the threshold. When the wolf saw me, he bared his teeth and I briefly wondered whether showing fangs meant the same thing for werewolves as it did for vampires. I wasn't really down for doggie style in the sheriff's office.

"Down, boy," I said.

The wolf snarled.

"Sheriff, it's me," I said, backing away slowly. "It's your buddy, Rose. We shared cracklewhip chowder at the Lighthouse, remember? It was a good time. You made fun of me for not sharing your spoon."

The wolf advanced toward me, still looking angry and ready to attack.

"We're sort of friends," I continued. "You let me do weird things like drink bourbon in your office."

"He let you drink the bourbon in his office?" an incredulous voice asked.

I jerked my head to see Deputy Bolan, aiming a crossbow at the sheriff-turned-werewolf. "Crap on a stick. What do you think you're doing?"

"You know, your limited range of colorful language is wholly unimpressive for someone from New Jersey," the leprechaun said.

"You're choosing now to criticize my lack of curse words?"

"You're staring down the face of an angry wolf," he said. "If ever there was a time to curse, it's now."

"It's because of Marley," I said. "I made a conscious effort when she was little to avoid bad language as much as possible. Now it's a habit."

Saliva dripped from the wolf's jaws.

"You can't kill the sheriff," I said hotly.

"I'm not going to kill him," the deputy replied. "It's a tran-quilizer for this very occasion."

"You guys are better equipped for monster emergencies than I ever imagined," I said.

Deputy Bolan bristled. "Don't call my boss a monster." He fired and hit the wolf square in the chest. The lupine sheriff yelped before collapsing on the floor in a heap of thick fur.

I made a move toward him, but the deputy grabbed my arm.

"Not yet," he said. "We need to make sure he's really out."

"He'd pretend?" I queried.

"Not necessarily, but if he's awake, he can bite."

My skin tingled with fear. "So what do we do?"

"Just stand here another minute, then we'll call in a team to help move him to a secure cell."

My head snapped toward the leprechaun. "A cell?"

"Like your vampire buddy. He can't roam around town as an angry wolf," Deputy Bolan said. "Can you imagine the backlash?"

"He'd be horrified if he hurt someone," I said.

"That he would." The deputy pulled out his phone and sent a text. "You can go, Ember. I have plenty of people on hand to help."

I stared at the unconscious wolf on the floor. He looked so unlike his usual self, so vulnerable. "I don't feel right about leaving."

"There's nothing you can do for him," Deputy Bolan said. "I need to contain him until he reverts back to human form. Then we'll figure out what triggered the change."

"It was very unexpected," I said. "We were sitting there talking and he shifted."

The leprechaun rubbed his head. "And Alec Hale went full vamp. Something strange is happening."

A moment later a team of elves swarmed the room, lifting the wolf onto a stretcher and carrying him out of the room.

"Where are they taking him?" I asked.

"Come on," the deputy said. "I'll show you."

I followed him down a long corridor to a circular staircase. We spiraled down until the staircase emptied out into a large room. The elves were already in the process of leaving.

"The sheriff's in here," the deputy said. "Alec is in the room next door." He pointed to the doorway where the elves had just passed through.

The sheriff's wolf form was locked behind a silver door with a small barred window at knee level. Clearly, they'd had use for a werewolf cell before. The wolf's chest rose and fell. I sighed with relief. Definitely not dead.

"I'm so sorry, Sheriff," I said. "I don't know what happened."

Unsurprisingly, there was no response.

"Would you mind if I checked on Alec?" I asked.

"Be quick about it," the deputy said.

I walked hesitantly into the room and peered through the narrow slit in the cell door. Alec sat on a stool, staring into the void.

"You shouldn't be here, Miss Rose," he said darkly.

"How did you know I was here?"

"Vampire hearing, remember?" He refused to look at me.

"I want to make sure you're okay," I said.

"I shall be much improved when you're no longer here."

Ouch.

"Did I do something...?"

"Miss Rose," he interrupted. His voice was calm but firm.

"What?"

78

He hastened a look at me. "'What' is not really the proper response. It is more polite to say 'yes, Mr. Hale.'"

I cleared my throat with as much sarcasm as I could inject into a single sound. "Yes, Alec?"

He forced his attention back to the stone wall. "I can feel the vibrations of your beating heart. It would be best if you left. Truly. I'm very strong. I might try to escape." He swallowed hard. "Trust me. Neither of us wants that outcome."

"Alec, the sheriff turned into a wolf right in front of me. Something strange is going on. Let me help you."

His jaw tensed and I caught a glimpse of his fang. "Please, Miss Rose. You must go. The smell of your blood stirs my own."

I pressed my palm flat against the door. I hated how powerless I felt.

"I'm sorry," I said, and fled the room before I was faced once again with the monster from the newspaper office.

Deputy Bolan caught sight of me as I rushed from the room. "Are you all right, Ember?"

"Fine," I said, and heard the quiver in my voice. Whether I wanted to admit it or not, the sight of Alec had frightened me. His restraint was remarkable, but the realization that he wanted to rip out my throat overshadowed everything else.

The deputy followed me back up the circular staircase.

"How's the sheriff?" I asked, pulling myself together.

"Still lupine," the deputy replied. "I'm hoping he shifts back overnight."

"Me, too." Even though he was a werewolf, it must have scared him to realize he was trapped in a single form. He spent most of his time as human, shifting at will. This had to be a nightmare for him.

A nightmare.

I closed my eyes, absorbing the reality of the situation.

"Never fear," the deputy said. "Things are under control.

Go home and have one of your aunt's famous cocktails. I've got things covered here."

"If you're sure." I needed to go home and think.

"Quite sure. You have other jobs to focus on, like a daughter that will need to be picked up from school later."

"Yes, there's always something." And no way would I tell Marley about the day's events. She'd have her own nightmares for weeks. She liked and trusted both men, especially Alec.

"Keep what happened under your hat. We don't need hysteria. I promise I'll let you know if anything changes," he said.

"Why would you do that?" I asked. Deputy Bolan was barely tolerant of me most of the time.

"Because you seem to care."

"Of course I care," I said hotly. "I don't know what you think of me…"

"It doesn't matter what I think of you," the deputy interjected. "Right now my priority is the sheriff. Like I said, I'll be in touch."

I didn't like the way the leprechaun looked at me, as though this was somehow my fault. I mustered the remaining energy I had and left the building without another word.

CHAPTER 9

I FELT TOO SHAKEN by the day's events to go straight home. Marley was in school for another hour and a half, so I had a little time to decompress. I *needed* to decompress. What were the odds that both men would release their inner demons in my presence on the same day? As much as I tried to dismiss the connection, I couldn't ignore the fact that I was also with Bentley and Trupti when their worst fears came to life. And Milo Jarvis. What if somehow *I* was the common denominator? I didn't understand my magic yet. Maybe I was more powerful than I realized. What if Wren was right and I was a natural—but a natural *what*? Was I somehow responsible for this awful curse?

I left the hustle and bustle of town and headed through the woods until I heard the call of the ocean. Some people liked birdsong or falling rain. For me, the ocean was the most soothing sound in the world. I didn't realize how calming its gentle rhythm was until this moment.

I reached the coastal path and kept walking until I spotted Kirby's Kayaks on one of the docks on Balefire Beach. I'd never been in a kayak before. The idea was appealing.

"Hey, Kirby," I said, greeting the woman on the dock. She was pretty, with auburn hair that stretched past her bottom.

"Actually, my name is Sela," she replied.

"Oh, I thought you might be the owner," I said.

"I am. I wanted alliteration for the company name, so I used Kirby in honor of my hamster."

A kayak company named after a hamster. Why not?

"Nice to meet you, Sela. I'm Ember and I'd like to rent a kayak."

She sniffed the salty air. "I don't smell the sea on you. Have you ever been kayaking before?"

"No, but I spent plenty of summers at the beach." What did she mean she didn't smell the sea on me?

Sela scrutinized me. "Half an hour or an hour? Let's say half an hour. Your arms look weak."

"Okay, so upper body strength is not my forte. No need to be mean."

"Sorry." She gave me a sheepish grin. "Sometimes my thoughts slide right off my tongue."

I could certainly relate to that.

Thankfully, I had just enough cash on me to pay for the half an hour. An hour would have been too much.

Sela was very patient with me and explained how to paddle, how to turn, and why it was important to move parallel to the coastline.

After the brief tutorial, I slid into the yellow kayak and gripped the paddles. What was I thinking? I sat perfectly still, unable to move. With my luck, I'd probably attract a shark. Was that a worst fear for me? Although it would suck, it probably didn't qualify. I was always more concerned with bad things happening to Marley than to me.

"Don't waste time sitting next to the dock," Sela said. "Get out there and mingle with the ocean." She pushed the end of the kayak with her foot and sent me gliding across the water.

"Popcorn balls," I yelled, as the water splashed over me. Despite the lesson, I wasn't very adept with the paddles. On a positive note, my incompetence forced me to focus on not capsizing and drowning, so I stopped worrying about the sheriff, Alec, and the nightmare curse. There was something to be said for physical exertion to take your mind off your troubles. Hmm. Maybe if I cleaned more often, my mind would be clearer.

Nah. Probably not.

The waves began to roll higher and the kayak dipped from side to side. It was both exciting and unsettling. I was so close to the water, it felt like I was one with the waves. I'd have to come back with Marley one day. Seeing how much she enjoyed her magical boogie board, I knew she'd love this, too.

"You're getting the hang of it," a voice said.

I glanced in the water beside me to see Sela's auburn head bobbing in the waves. "Is it safe for you to swim out here? Aren't you worried about riptides?" Or sharks.

Sela laughed. "I'm definitely not worried about riptides." Her head disappeared and, the next thing I knew, a pair of green flippers broke the surface before slipping beneath the waves.

"Sweet baby Ariel," I said, staring at the place in the water where the tail disappeared. "Sela's a mermaid."

I wasn't sure why that fact surprised me. Not after arriving in Starry Hollow. Not after today.

"Are there any creatures in the water here I should worry about?" I called.

Sela's head popped back up next to me. "There's nothing to fear. Most creatures of the deep wish you no harm."

"No Krakens then?"

"Word in the water is that they're extinct," Sela said. "I've spent my whole life in these waters and I've never seen one."

Small favors.

"You might see a selkie, but they're harmless," she said. "Like mermaids."

I stopped moving the paddles. "What's a selkie?"

Sela smiled. "You don't know what they are? How interesting."

"I'm from the human world," I said. "I'm still figuring out all these paranormal types." And Marley wasn't here to educate me.

"Selkies are much like us. They live as seals in the water, and as humans on land."

I continued to paddle alongside her and winced when I smacked my hand on the side of the kayak. This would definitely take practice.

"Oh, but if you hear a beautiful singing voice, paddle quickly in the opposite direction," Sela warned.

"That's an odd directive."

She smiled. "I suppose you've never heard of sirens either."

"No, I have heard of those," I said. "My daughter told me about them. Some guy tied himself to a pole on his ship to avoid swimming to them."

"One of many stories," Sela said. "Most of them are fully integrated in society, although we do get the occasional rogue siren that decides to have fun with people on the water." She shook her head in disgust.

"I'll keep an ear out," I said.

Sela floated on her back beside the kayak. "Why do I get the sense you came out here to escape something?"

"Not escape," I said. "Just think clearly. Bad stuff happened today and I feel like it's my fault."

"We women do carry an acute sense of responsibility," Sela said. She smacked her tail flat on the water, sending water droplets in all directions. "Or perhaps you're a narcissist."

"Probably a little of both," I admitted.

Sela dipped her tail back into the water. "Whatever the problem is, try taking yourself out of the equation and see if you can find a solution that doesn't include you. That might help you determine where the fault actually belongs."

I stared at her in awe. "What are you? Some kind of water therapist?"

"Unofficially," she replied. "You seem very at home out here. Perhaps you were meant for the sea after all."

I looked at the coastline in the distance and sighed. "I do like it. It's peaceful and quiet." And as much as I wanted to stay longer, I knew it was time to head for shore. "Thanks for the pep talk, Sela. I'm sure I'll see you again."

"I'll meet you back at the dock," she said. "With those arms, I suspect you'll have trouble getting yourself out of the kayak."

I couldn't help but laugh. "Thanks, I think." I turned the kayak around and followed the mermaid back to the dock. Although my problem wasn't resolved, at least I felt better about it. That was the most I could hope for right now.

I decided to take Sela's advice and remove myself from the equation. See if I could find another plausible reason for the curses. To that end, I returned to the sheriff's office the next day, ready for action. Deputy Bolan sat behind the sheriff's desk. I briefly wondered how high he had to raise the seat in order to see over the top of the desk.

"What brings you back so soon?" Deputy Bolan asked, eyeing me curiously. "I told you I'd be in touch."

I dropped into one of the chairs. "I'm being proactive like any good reporter would."

The leprechaun pumped his tiny green fist in the air. "Good for you." His scowl quickly reappeared. "Now why are you here?"

I leaned on the desk. "Why don't you like me?"

"Because you're annoying. Next question."

"You hardly know me."

"Don't need to. Our first meeting was evidence enough." He went back to examining the papers on his desk.

"I want to help you figure out what's going on with Alec and Sheriff Nash," I said.

He peered at me. "Why? Worried you won't have a date for Friday night if those two are still locked up downstairs?"

I bristled. "I'm not dating either one of them."

Deputy Bolan pointed a slender finger at me. "Let's keep it that way."

"What's it to you?" I demanded. "You're not married to either of them, unless there's something no one is telling me."

He looked ready to nip me with his little leprechaun teeth. "I'm already married, thank you very much. My husband's name is Declan. He's an art teacher at the elementary school."

"See?" I said. "No reason to get your knickers in a twist. You're all set."

"What's in it for you?" Deputy Bolan asked. "Another byline? Doesn't one byline meet your quota for the year?"

"Just because my aunt got me the job doesn't mean I don't take it seriously," I said. "When the sheriff and the editor-in-chief of the local paper are both impacted by some type of curse, that's newsworthy."

"I'm starting to think your vampire is cursed in general. It seems like only yesterday he was a frog."

"He is a bit of a damsel in distress, isn't he?" I smothered a laugh. Alec would die all over again if he'd heard me say that. "The damsel needs our help, and so does the sheriff."

Deputy Bolan heaved a sigh. "I can tell you'll only leave here by force. So what do you propose?"

"I thought you could review the list of recent arrests. See if there are any magic users or someone known to dabble in magic-for-hire."

"You think someone wants revenge on the sheriff?" he queried. "But that doesn't explain the other affected parties."

"No, but it's a start. If someone's gone willy-nilly with magic, maybe the sheriff already caught part of the show without realizing it."

"That's..." The deputy hesitated. "That's actually a good idea." His chair swiveled in front of the computer and his tiny fingers hammered away on the keyboard. "I'll pull up a list now."

"Look at us—working as a team. The sheriff would be so proud."

"Don't get ahead of yourself." Deputy Bolan scanned the screen. "Here's a good one. I remember this guy. A wizard we arrested last week."

"A wizard from my coven?" It still sounded weird to hear myself say 'my coven.'

"Yep. An older fella called Montague. The sheriff arrested him for practicing magic in a public space without a permit."

"That *is* a good lead. Where was he arrested?"

"In front of Muse Fountain. He was trying to change the moving statutes into real women. Pygmalion style."

"Just for fun?"

"He was drunk, apparently. It was two in the morning and he'd spent the better part of the evening in Elixir."

"So why not charge him with drunk and disorderly?" I asked.

Deputy Bolan shrugged. "I guess we'll need to ask the wizard because I don't speak wolf."

"Anyone else?" I asked.

Deputy Bolan continued to read the screen and frowned. "Oh, I remember this one. A fairy called Desdemona. She was released on bail."

"A fairy makes sense," I said.

"And she had an attitude, that one. I had to wrestle her wand away."

"And you managed to get it? How small was this fairy?" Maybe her name should be Thumbelina.

The leprechaun scowled. "I'm capable of disarming a suspect, thank you very much. It's in the job description."

"Okay," I said. "Add her to the short list." I cringed. "Sorry. I didn't mean to say 'short' list. We'll pay her a visit, too."

The deputy shook his head. "I'm beginning to rethink this team effort."

"Don't knock it 'til you try it," I said. "The sheriff and I have done pretty well with it so far."

Deputy Bolan bristled. "*I'm* his team. You're nothing but a wannabe reporter."

I rolled my eyes. "Fine, Deputy. We won't be a team. We'll just parallel play like two toddlers. Sound good?"

"Is that another short joke?"

I smacked my forehead. "Don't look for insults that aren't there. Trust me, mine are pretty stinkin' obvious."

"At least that's one thing we agree on, Ember," he said.

"What's that?" I asked.

"There's nothing subtle about you."

CHAPTER 10

Montague lived in the section of town known as the Breezeway. I figured out pretty quickly where the name came from. The wind whipped my hair around my face, dragging thin strands into my mouth. Delightful.

"You didn't inherit the glorious head of Rose hair, did you?" Deputy Bolan queried. He observed my hair from a safe distance as it continued to torture me by slapping my eyeballs.

I tugged the wayward strands out of my mouth. "No, apparently not."

"Why don't you pull it back in a ponytail or something?"

"The individual strands are too thin," I explained. "There is no hairband or barrette on earth that can contain this hair. It's like Houdini. It escapes every attempt at containment."

"Who's Houdini?"

"Forget it," I said.

We stepped up to the door and I let Deputy Bolan take the lead. I wanted to stay on the leprechaun's good side so he didn't change his mind about teamwork. It seemed to take a few minutes for the occupant to register the knock on the door, but eventually the wizard came around. He looked around sixty-five years old, silver hair, with a matching beard and mustache. He wore a navy blue robe with white stars and his legs were bare, suggesting there wasn't much beneath the robe. I sure hoped that belt kept everything under wraps during our visit.

"What's this?" Montague asked. "I didn't know the sheriff's office did follow-up visits."

"May we come in?" Deputy Bolan asked.

Montague glanced over his shoulder, as though checking something. "I suppose I'll allow it."

He left the door open and retreated into the house. The inside of the bungalow was a mess, to put it mildly. There were stacks of newspaper, books, and magazines on every available surface space. I noticed several used mugs on the coffee table. The beady eyes of a creature peered out from beneath the sofa.

"Do you have a pet, Montague?" I asked. I really, really prayed he had a pet.

He looked thoughtful for a moment. "Oh, you must mean Libby."

"Green eyes?" I queried.

He nodded, scratching his beard. "Yes, she was my wife's familiar."

Hallelujah.

"Can I offer you a light refreshment?" he asked. "Maybe a cup of tea or coffee? I think I have sugar left, though I haven't been paying close attention."

Observing the state of the place, I didn't think Montague was paying close attention to much of anything these days. I was hesitant to accept food or drink from the wizard, no matter how sweet he seemed.

"Have you been drinking again, Montague?" Deputy Bolan asked.

Montague didn't react. "What I do in the privacy of my own home is my business."

I followed the leprechaun's gaze and realized why he'd asked the question. Peeking out from the kitchen counter were several empty bottles of ale.

"Where's your wife, Montague?" I asked.

He met my inquisitive gaze. "Dead. Seven years next month."

"I'm sorry," I said. "I didn't realize." I thought maybe she had just gone away to visit a relative or something. There seemed to be a woman's touch beneath the clutter. In fact, women's shoes were visible underneath the settee. I didn't dare ask if they were Montague's.

"Who are you?" he asked me. "I don't recognize you."

"I'm Ember Rose," I said. "I'm helping out the deputy."

"Rose," he repeated. "One of *the* Roses?"

"I guess you've missed all the coven events that mentioned my arrival."

"I'm sure I have. I rarely socialize anymore. The coven brings back too many memories of my wife." He lowered his head. "She was very active in the coven. Served as the Bard before Camille."

"You're not missing much," I said. "Lots of financial reports on fundraisers." I pretended to yawn.

"So what's this visit for?" Montague asked. "Have you brought me a pamphlet? Come to tell me about a meeting I can join? Don't bother. I've heard it all before."

Deputy Bolan perched on the arm of the sofa. I guess he liked to remain as high as possible given his short stature. I took his cue and sat on the settee.

"We'd just like to follow up with you on your recent arrest," the deputy said. "We were wondering why the sheriff charged you with practicing magic without a permit instead of drunk and disorderly."

Montague smoothed his beard. "The sheriff didn't tell you?"

"He's incommunicado at the moment," Deputy Bolan replied. I could understand why he wasn't willing to say more. The last thing we needed was the whole town freaking out because the sheriff was incapacitated.

"Sheriff Nash was being kind," Montague said. "If he'd charged me with drunk and disorderly, it would have been my third offense this year. There would have been more serious consequences than a slap on the wrist."

"What kind of magic were you practicing at the fountain at two in the morning?" I asked.

"A transformation spell," he replied.

Deputy Bolan and I exchanged looks. It could have been a transformation spell rather than a nightmare curse that changed the sheriff into his wolf form.

"What were you trying to transform?" the deputy asked.

Montague studied the carpet fibers. "The statues. The ones in the fountain."

"The ones that move?" I queried. Marley and I had noticed them from the sky during our broomstick tour when we first moved to town.

He nodded. "I thought that if I could change at least one of them into human form, I could have a few hours of companionship."

"You were trying to turn them into humans?" I asked. "Is that even possible?"

The older wizard shrugged. "Don't know. I was drunk enough to try, though. I was a talented wizard once upon a time."

A calico paw popped out from beneath the sofa.

"Does she ever come out from under there?" I asked.

Montague glanced at the roving paw. "On occasion. She misses my wife." He heaved a sigh. "So do I."

My morning latte from the Caffeinated Cauldron worked its way through my system faster than normal. "Excuse me. Do you mind if I use your bathroom?"

Montague motioned with his hand. "Down the hall. Second door on the left."

I hurried down the hall, noting the framed photographs that hung on the wall. Montague and his wife enjoying various vacations. Both smiling happily for the camera. Fixed points in time when they didn't know it would come to an abrupt end. I understood his pain.

I slipped into the bathroom and the first thing I noticed was the presence of women's perfume on the shelf above the towel rail. There was also a woman's robe hanging on the back of the door and a second toothbrush on the sink. Why was Montague looking for a companion when he clearly already had one? The bathroom was surprisingly clean for a room with so much clutter. It had to be magic. Based on Montague's depressed state, I highly doubted he bothered with a toilet brush.

I finished quickly in the bathroom and returned to the living area. Libby was now stretched out beneath the sofa, her bottom half still hidden from view. She was slowly getting used to us.

"I don't mean to pry," I said, "but why were you bothering to turn statues into humans when it appears that you already have a woman staying with you?"

He gave me a blank look. "There's no one staying with me except Libby."

I gestured to the bathroom. "You have a woman's robe in your bathroom. And a second toothbrush."

He appeared momentarily confused. "Those belong to my wife."

I tilted my head. "You said she died seven years ago."

"That's right," he replied. "And I keep everything as it was the day she died. She still has her half of the closet, too. And her reading glasses on the bedside table." He smiled vaguely. "There's an unfinished crossword that I occasionally itch to complete. I can't bear the thought of it being finished, though, so I leave it."

A lump formed in my throat. It took a lot to make me cry, but I could easily have succumbed to tears in that moment. I dug my fingernails into the palm of my hand to keep my emotions in check.

"Montague, do you mean to tell me that you left your wife's belongings exactly as they were for the last seven years?" The deputy looked aghast.

"What do you expect me to do?" he asked. "Throw them all away? Erase her memory forever? What kind of husband would I be if I did such a thing?"

Libby crawled the rest of the way out from under the sofa and stared at me with her big green eyes. Her loneliness was palpable.

"What about your familiar?" I asked. "Libby belonged to your wife. Don't you have one of your own?"

"My familiar died three years ago. Feline leukemia. It's been Libby and me ever since. She never liked me much, though. My wife and I could never understand it."

I glanced at the calico cat. "Have you considered rehoming her?" I wasn't sure what the protocol was for orphaned familiars. Was it the same as rehoming a regular cat?

"I don't think Libby would thrive in another house," he said. "She's lived in this bungalow most of her life."

I reached down to let the cat sniff my hand. Although I wasn't a cat person like Marley, they didn't tend to hate me.

"Do you think your wife would be happy to know that Libby was lonely?" I asked. "That you were lonely? Surely she would've wanted you both to let go and find new sources of happiness." As soon as the words came out of my mouth, I pictured Marley's wagging finger in my face. *I could say the same to you.*

Montague looked down at the cat, as though seeing her for the first time. "I make sure to feed her and give her water. Even a bowl of milk on Christmas, like my wife used to do. She's cared for."

"But she isn't loved, Montague," I said. "Not the way she deserves to be. The same goes for you. How is getting drunk and practicing magic going to help you climb out of this hole?" I didn't want to imagine how long it had been going on. Seven years of this... I dreaded the thought.

I ran my hand down Libby's soft back. Montague was right about one thing—she was well cared for. Her coat was still healthy and shiny. If I believed that PP3 could handle another major change in his life, I would have offered to bring her home with me.

"Montague, if I can find a good home for Libby, would you consider letting her go?" I asked.

He dug his fingers into his silver beard. "I'll have to think about it."

I nodded, understanding. "Okay, if I find someone, I'll let you know and you can decide then." I felt a sudden pang of longing for Miss Kowalski, my former neighbor. It occurred to me that not only would she adopt Libby in a heartbeat, she'd also be good company for Montague. Too bad New Jersey was so far away.

"Thanks for your time," Deputy Bolan said. "And if you're interested, I do have a list of meetings that you might want to consider attending. They're a great way to get yourself out of the house and meet people."

Montague nodded absently. He looked so forlorn, standing in the middle of the living room in his robe. "I'll think about it," was all he said.

Deputy Bolan and I left the bungalow together. We walked back to the car without a snarky word, a first for the two of us.

"He's not our guy," I said, breaking the silence.

The deputy gave his head a sad shake. "No, he certainly isn't."

I pulled in front of Palmetto House and lingered in my new sports car, a gift from Florian that I named Sylvia.

"Mom, can we go in?"

I held up a finger. The last refrain of Madonna's *Borderline* was blasting from the speakers.

"Mom," Marley huffed. "You can hear it again on the way home if you want. Let's go in. I want to see my cousins."

I turned off the engine. "Fine. I'll remember this the next time you want to finish a page in your book before coming to dinner or brushing your teeth for bed."

Marley suddenly seemed to realize she'd acted against her best interest. "It *is* a good song."

"Nope. Too late. Let's go in."

We climbed the dual staircase out front and met at the front door. Marley beat me by two strides.

"Your legs get longer every day," I said. "You're going to be tall like your father."

"How tall was Daddy?" she asked.

"Six foot four," I replied, and opened the door without knocking. The front door of the inn was usually unlocked thanks to the coming and going of its guests.

"Perfect timing," Linnea said. My cousin was in the main living space of the inn, adding fresh flowers to a vase. "We're all downstairs. Fair warning, though. Wyatt's here."

I arched an eyebrow. "Why?"

"He's upset about Granger and wanted to see the kids, so Bryn invited him to stay for dinner."

I gave her a sympathetic smile. "Don't worry. I've got your back."

Marley and I followed Linnea to their living quarters on the lower level. Sure enough, Wyatt was playing catch with Hudson in the middle of the room.

"Wyatt Nash, please stop throwing a ball in the house this instant," Linnea yelled, her hands glued to her hips. No one seemed to rile my cousin like her ex-husband. It was a gift.

Wyatt chuckled and dropped the ball to the floor. "Sorry, I forget about all your rules."

"My rules," Linnea scoffed. "You mean the ones like don't have relationships with other women during the marriage? Those rules?"

Wyatt groaned. "Here we go. Can't we just have a nice family dinner without the nagging and arguing?"

Linnea's nostrils flared and her fingers twitched. I had the feeling she was about to hex his furry werewolf butt.

"Linnea, can I help you in the kitchen?" I interjected.

"Mom, leave it to the experts," Marley said.

I fixed her with a hard stare. "Thanks for your support, daughter."

"That would be great, Ember. Thanks." Linnea gathered her wits and headed to the kitchen, leaving Wyatt to tackle Hudson to the floor in what was likely an illegal wrestling move.

Once we were safely ensconced in the kitchen, Linnea retrieved her starter wand from a nearby drawer.

"Feel like practicing?" she asked.

"Oh, your mother didn't tell you?" I whipped out my new wand and showed her.

Linnea admired the silver sheen. "Very pretty. Did Mother approve?"

"In her vague way." I gripped the wand and steadied my breathing, letting the magical energy flow from my body to the wand.

"I wasn't sure whether she would let you start on wandwork yet."

"I think Marigold spoke to her," I said. "She knows I'm getting itchy feet." I wiggled the wand. "Or fingers."

"It's understandable. You have a lot of power flowing through those veins of yours. It needs a release."

"Should I try and prepare food?" I asked.

Linnea considered the suggestion. "Maybe stick with setting the table for now. Food takes more skill, especially when you're serving it to six people."

"Fair enough. So do you want the good china?"

Linnea shook her head. "Not when Wyatt's here. Too many meals have ended with a dish getting thrown across the room." She hesitated. "After the children have gone to bed, of course."

I focused my will on the wand. "Napkin dreams and cutlery wishes/bring out six serving dishes."

Linnea and I watched in silence as the drawers and doors of the hutch opened and the requested items drifted to the table.

"Nice work," Linnea said. "You're a natural."

I tried not to react to the word 'natural,' especially when I knew she intended it as a compliment. Now wasn't the time to share my fear over my possible connection to the nightmare curse.

"Of course, she's a natural. She's a Rose," Bryn said, appearing in the kitchen doorway. I noticed Marley hovering behind her. "Can Marley and I play Scrabble?"

"After dinner," Linnea said. "We're going to eat shortly."

The girls wore matching crestfallen expressions as they retreated to the living room.

"It's so great that Marley has an older cousin with similar interests," I said. "I hated that she had no one back in New Jersey. Her best friend was Miss Kowalski, the older woman who babysat her after school."

"It's great for Bryn, too," Linnea said. "She and Hudson seem to argue nonstop. Having Marley here is an instant buffer."

"Wyatt seems to be a buffer, too," I said.

Linnea's pretty face soured. "Yes, but his presence creates a whole new set of arguments." She pressed her fingertips against the oven door and closed her eyes.

"What are you doing?" I asked.

"Making a pot roast."

"But there wasn't anything in the oven," I said.

"There is now," Linnea said with a smile.

"Ooh. Can you add those little white potatoes?" I asked. "I love them."

Linnea touched the oven door again and muttered something under her breath. "Wyatt loves those, too." She clapped her hands and a bottle of wine appeared on the counter in front of her. "Pinot noir?"

"Sure."

"Yum, something smells delicious." Wyatt strode into the kitchen, wearing a lopsided grin that reminded me of his brother. I pushed the image of the sheriff's limp lupine body from my mind.

"Pot roast is ready," Linnea said.

Wyatt's brow lifted. "You trying to butter me up? You know that's my favorite."

"You're upset about Granger. I want to cheer you up." Linnea poured a glass of wine and handed it to Wyatt.

"You maybe wanna use a bigger glass for me?" Wyatt asked. He handed me the stemmed wine glass. "I'll have it in a pint glass with ice."

Linnea cringed. "Of course you will." She plucked a pint glass from the cupboard and filled it with ice before pouring the wine. "Stay classy, Wyatt."

"Sorry," Wyatt said, slurping his wine. "We can't all be as fancy as the Rose-Muldoons."

"I'm still working on it," I admitted. "I'm pretty sure it's out of my wheelhouse."

"Nonsense," Linnea said. "You fit right in."

Wyatt snickered. "Really? Miss Mafia Princess fits right in with the hoity-toity white-blond brigade?"

"I'm not a mafia princess," I said hotly. The mere suggestion of being associated with the mafia sent shivers up my spine. The whole reason I was in Starry Hollow was because of a crazed mobster.

"Wyatt, I'm tolerating your presence here tonight because of your brother," Linnea said. "Don't make me regret it."

Wyatt set his pint glass on the counter. "You're right, babe. I'm sorry. I've got a lot of pent-up frustration and nowhere to focus it. I wish the moon was full."

"You can't turn if there's no full moon?" I asked.

"I can, but there are requirements on off nights," he said. "A bunch of bureaucratic minotaur shit. Our movements are more restricted."

"So you'd rather get drunk and find some willing bimbo to take home instead," Linnea said. "In other words, Tuesday."

"Ha ha," Wyatt drawled. "I obviously didn't marry you for your sense of humor."

"Because you have none," Linnea shot back.

Hudson entered the kitchen, a pained expression on his face. "Mom, I'm starving. Can we please eat?"

Wyatt grabbed the boy around the shoulders and squeezed. "You heard your growing werewolf son. He demands sustenance."

"I do," Hudson said weakly. "I'm famished."

"He's wasting away as we speak," Wyatt said, grinning.

Linnea glared at him before removing the pot roast from the oven. "Get your sister and Marley, please."

Hudson turned around and cupped his hands over his mouth. "Marley! Stink Breath! Dinnertime." He turned back to his mother and smiled. "Done."

Linnea snapped her fingers and the food made its way to the table. We brought our wine glasses with us.

The children seated themselves quickly, proving their claims of hunger were genuine. Linnea placed Wyatt at the opposite end of the table, as far from her as physically possible. Smart move.

"What do you think happened to the sheriff to make him a permanent wolf?" Marley asked.

"No idea," Wyatt replied, going to town on his slice of the pot roast. With those table manners, I didn't know how he managed to survive Sunday dinners at Thornhold for as long as he did.

"Do you think he's happier in his wolf form?" Marley asked.

"Not Granger," Wyatt said. "It's not his way. He likes being the sheriff and that requires his human form more often than anything."

"You should go and see him," I said. "He'd probably feel better if he saw his brother."

Wyatt fixated on his plate. "I don't know. It'll be hard seeing him like that."

"But you love the wolf form," I said. "Why is it hard?"

"Like I said, Granger's not as much of a fan." His expression clouded over. "I don't wanna see my brother miserable."

"Wyatt's an avoider," Linnea said. "He doesn't like to confront situations that make him uncomfortable." *One of the many reasons our marriage failed.*

At first, I thought Linnea had said that last part out loud. It took me a moment to realize I'd heard her thoughts. I chewed my pot roast, listening for more. Between Hudson's ADHD-style thoughts and the girls' apparent contemplation of the state of the universe while enjoying potatoes, there was too much noise to filter through, so I gave up. Wyatt's was the only mind I couldn't read at all, and I wondered whether it was because he shielded it or because there simply wasn't anything there to read.

"Dinner is delicious, Linnea," Marley said. "I love gravy."

"As long as she can drown her food in gravy or ketchup, she's okay," I explained.

"Thank you, darling," Linnea replied. "I'm glad you like it."

Marley glanced at Wyatt, who'd cleared his plate. "If you don't want to see your brother alone, I'll go with you."

Wyatt appeared taken aback. "You will? Well, that's awfully sweet of you."

"I like Sheriff Nash," Marley said. "I want him to be okay. And Alec, too."

I patted her hand on the table. "Don't worry, sweetheart. They will be."

I hoped.

CHAPTER 11

WREN and I stood in a clearing in the woods, ready for my first official incantation lesson. Now that I had my cloak and starter wand, I was beginning to feel more like a true member of the coven instead of a New Jersey woman on a weird vacation.

"We're going to start easy today," Wren said. "Let you get comfortable with the wand. First, we'll try a locking spell and then an unlocking spell."

I glanced around at the live oaks. "Exactly what am I unlocking in the middle of the woods? The key to your heart?"

He clutched his chest. "Oh, Ember. I'm afraid you've misread me. You're pretty and all, but I wouldn't go near a Rose. Too much pressure."

"That's a little unfair," I said, thinking of Alec's similar sentiment. "What if you really liked me?"

He shook his head. "Wouldn't be enough to survive what-ever torture your aunt would put me through."

"But she'd be thrilled. She *wants* me to date a wizard."

He pointed to himself. "Not this wizard. Besides, you're being way too forward to make me think you're serious."

"Yeah. I'm messing with you. Sorry. I would never date a wizard just to please my aunt."

He cocked an eyebrow. "What about to please yourself?"

"I'm good right now, but thanks."

"So how about we focus on this instead?" He pointed his wand at the nearest tree and said, "*Ostium.*"

A door appeared at the base of the enormous tree.

"That'll do," I said.

"So glad you approve." He grinned. "Now, I believe you've already been instructed on how to focus your will."

"I have."

"Excellent. Then you simply point your wand at the lock, focus your will, and say *obfirmo.*"

"Sounds easy enough." I cleared my throat and placed my body in the spell-casting position. "*Obfirmo.*"

"You don't need to yell it," Wren said.

"I wasn't yelling," I replied.

"You weren't?" He pretended to clean out his ears. "Maybe try your inside voice."

"But we're *outside.*"

"Listen, when you're advanced enough, you won't even need to say it out loud."

"My cousin said that I won't need a wand either," I said. "I'll be able to snap my fingers or wiggle my pinky or something and make stuff happen."

"That's entirely possible given your lineage." He inclined his head toward the door. "But first let's master a basic spell with your starter wand."

"Shouldn't we unlock it now?" I asked.

"Shouldn't you make sure you actually locked it first?" He strode toward the door and tugged on the handle. The door opened without resistance.

"Oh." My lips straightened in disappointment. "I'll have to try again."

"Good idea." He folded his arms and watched me as I performed the spell again.

"You don't need to look so smug," I said. "It's distracting."

"My smugness is distracting?" he repeated. "That's one I haven't heard before. Usually, it's my good looks."

I snorted. "Sorry. Not indulging your ego."

"And why should you? I hear you've got a bevy of admirers already."

I paused and looked at him. "Where did you hear that?"

"Oh, come on. You have to know everyone talks in a small town like Starry Hollow. And you're a new witch from the human world. A long-lost Rose. People can't help but show an interest."

"I'm not that interesting," I said. "I put my deodorant on one armpit at a time like everybody else." I sniffed the air. "Except maybe you. I think you skipped today."

He gave me an amused look. "Antagonizing the teacher is not going to make the lesson go smoothly."

"I don't need the lesson to go smoothly. I have no use for locking and unlocking doors with a wand."

"You never know," he said. "You may find yourself in a dire situation where your very survival depends on your skill with a wand."

"Because Starry Hollow is so scary?"

His brow lifted. "It's my understanding that your boss nearly attacked you in a heightened vampire state."

"Where did you hear that?" I demanded. I thought we were trying to keep the information on a need-to-know basis.

"Like I said. Everyone talks." He waved a finger in the air and the door closed.

"Well, I don't see how a locking or unlocking spell would've helped me in that situation."

"You're missing the point, Ember." He sighed. "Go ahead and try again."

I'd show him. I pointed my wand, focused my will, and said, "*Obfirmo.*"

He tugged on the handle again. This time, it didn't budge. "Congratulations, Ember. You've successfully completed a skill that our eleven-year-olds master in their first week of school."

I stuck out my tongue.

"Careful," he warned. "I know a spell that rips those out."

I quickly sucked my tongue back in, unwilling to call his bluff. "So how do I unlock it?"

"Same thing, but say *dissere.*"

I managed the unlocking spell on the first try. Take that, Mr. Smug.

"Well done, Ember. Now there's no chance of locking yourself out of the house or your car."

"Unless I've forgotten my wand." Which was perfectly plausible.

He made a noise at the back of his throat. "Yes, I don't recommend it."

"Before we move on to changing the color of a butterfly or something, I have a question about a curse."

"A curse?"

"Not a curse like 'minotaur shit,'" I said. "I mean a hex."

He barked a sort laugh. "I know what you mean, Ember. I'm the Master-of-Incantation."

"How would someone create a curse that seems to make nightmares come true?"

"Depends."

"That's a lawyerly answer," I said. "Is it possible for a witch to curse people without knowing she did it?"

He peered at me. "Do you think you're somehow responsible for what happened to Alec?"

"I was with them all," I said.

"All?" he repeated. "How many have there been?"

"Never mind that. I've been trying to focus on other possibilities, but I'm concerned that I seem to be the common element."

He cocked his head, studying me. "I don't think so, Ember. I think you'd be aware if you were casting a spell of that magnitude."

"Then how do I explain it?"

"You don't," he replied simply. "It can't be you. Your magic may have potential, but you haven't fully accessed it."

"Then how does someone perform a nightmare curse? Do they find a spell in a book somewhere and copy it?"

He gave a thoughtful shrug. "It's possible. There are plenty of grimoires that contain curses. Or a more advanced witch or wizard could have created it from scratch. If it's a different type of magic user, maybe they've channeled dark magic somehow."

"That's a lot of options," I said. "How can we narrow it down?"

"You should let the sheriff and his team handle it," he said.

Ah, so he clearly didn't know about Sheriff Nash. That was good. No need to panic the townsfolk.

"I want to follow the story for *Vox Populi*," I said. "Alec would never forgive me if I didn't cover the story just because he was involved."

"You're fond of the vampire, aren't you?"

"He's a good boss," I said. "He could've decided I was a nuisance and left me to fetch coffee for everyone, but he didn't."

"Because he wants to stay on Hyacinth's good side, as do we all."

107

I shook my head. "No, it's more than that." I refused to say anything more out of respect for Alec. The vampire's admission was a private moment between the two of us and it was none of Wren's business.

"You should be careful around him, Ember," Wren said. "Even when he's at his most human, he's still a vampire."

"A polished, sophisticated, incredibly polite vampire that happens to believe in me."

Wren batted his eyelashes. "No wonder you're defending him. You're smitten."

"I'm not smitten," I objected. "No one gets smitten anymore. In fact, it's a proven fact that no one's been smitten since the 1800s."

Wren laughed. "You are a genuine delight to torture. Has anyone ever told you that?"

I glared at him. "What's the next spell?"

"A light spell," he said. "If you ever find yourself in a dark cave and can't see where you're going, this one comes in handy."

"I create light out of thin air?" I queried.

"No, it'll come from the tip of your wand." He tapped the end of mine.

I thought of Ashara and her amazing performance. "What about fire? Will I be able to manipulate it like I did the rain?"

"Too soon to tell," Wren said. "Why? Planning a forest fire? I don't recommend it. Some of these oaks are hundreds of years old."

"Of course not. I just think it would be cool to throw fire-balls," I said. "Very badass."

Wren gave me a thoughtful look before brandishing his wand. He pointed to a branch of a tree and said, "*Ambustio.*"

Flames sparked and the branch began to burn.

"What are you doing? You said these trees are old," I said.

"*Glaciare*," he said in an authoritative voice. The red and orange flames quickly turned blue and the branch iced over. "This branch was already dead. I wouldn't have done it otherwise."

A cracking sound drew my attention upward.

"Oops," he said. "Should've realized that would happen."

The frozen branch broke apart from the tree and plummeted toward our heads.

"*Vesica*," he said quickly.

The branched bounced off an invisible barrier and fell to the ground.

"What did you do?" I asked.

"I created a protective bubble around us," he said. "My brother taught me that one. He's the master when it comes to protective spells. Literally."

I reached out to touch the transparent roof above our heads. Although I felt resistance, I saw nothing.

"Okay, your class is definitely my favorite. Forget the flashlight spell. What's another cool one?"

"Changing the color of a butterfly, of course," he said. "That was your suggestion, wasn't it?"

I groaned. "It wasn't meant to be taken seriously."

"It's hard to tell with you. Fine, why don't we change the color of a leaf? Even easier since the leaf can't flutter away." He gave me the magic words and gestured to a leaf on the same tree as the door.

I focused my will, raised my wand, and said, "*Mutatio argenteus*."

I watched in amazement as every leaf on the tree turned a brilliant shade of silver. The tree sparkled in the sunlight.

Wren gazed at the tree with interest. "Very pretty. Not what I asked you to do, but a nice result all the same."

I dropped my arm to my side. "What did I do wrong?"

"Your focus wasn't narrow enough. You need to concentrate on that specific leaf, not all the leaves. It may not seem like an important distinction now, but there will come a time when it will be."

I nodded. "I need to change them back first. How do I do that? They weren't all the same exact color to start with."

"A reversal spell," Wren said. "*Rescindo.*"

I changed the leaves back to their original state and again focused on a single leaf. This time, only that leaf turned silver.

"There's hope for you yet, Ember," Wren said. "I like what I've seen so far."

"Are you sure you're not blowing sunshine up my cloak to please my aunt?"

He grinned and patted my shoulder. "You're on to me. Seriously, though, good job today. I wasn't sure whether the rumors were true."

I balked. "What rumors?"

"That you had some of that Rose talent."

"But how can you tell? You said eleven-year-olds completed these spells in their first week."

"And they do," he said. "But I wasn't talking about your magic." He winked and used his wand to make the door on the tree disappear. "Class is over today. I'll see you next time."

"Okay," I said, confused. What kind of talent did he mean?

Once Wren left, I plucked the silver leaf from the tree and brought it home as a souvenir to show Marley. She'd be thrilled to hear about my new spells. Her enthusiasm knew no bounds, which was one of the reasons I loved sharing things with her. She was able to express the excitement that I only felt.

On the walk back to the cottage, I thought about what Wren said regarding curses. It seemed that the field of possible culprits was wide open. And with so many different victims, it was difficult to figure out what the common denominator was. Despite Wren's opinion, as far as I was concerned, the common factor was still me.

CHAPTER 12

As we drove down Coastline Drive, Deputy Bolan informed me that Desdemona, the fairy with an attitude, was a tattoo artist that specialized in dragon art. With that nugget in mind, I expected the type of strip mall tattoo parlor that dotted the streets of New Jersey. *Desdemona's*, however, was a high-class establishment housed in a modern white building not far from the Whitethorn. There was a view of the ocean from the front of the building and Desdemona had wisely taken full advantage of that fact by placing the tattoo stations in the front rooms instead of the back.

"She must do good business," I murmured, checking out the expensive interior. The sleek furniture was stark white with clean lines and the floor was comprised of white tiles, giving it a clinical feel.

"Her dragon tattoos are legendary," Deputy Bolan said.

"Why? They're just tattoos," I said.

"Just tattoos," a voice repeated, incredulous.

I jerked my head toward the source of the sound. A fairy fluttered into the room, her short hair a deep shade of purple.

"They're *not* just tattoos?" I asked.

The fairy circled me, her white wings twitching. "Beautiful skin. Pull up your shirt. I can envision a red dragon on your torso."

I narrowed my eyes. "I don't pull up my shirt unless there's alcohol and a bet involved."

She smiled. "Desdemona Gilroy. Nice to meet you. I recognize Deputy McGreen Man over here from my recent visit to the slammer. Still can't believe you managed to take my wand. You're stronger than you look."

Deputy Bolan puffed out his chest. "You're speaking to the sheriff's deputy, Miss Gilroy. Try to show some respect."

The fairy rolled her eyes, unimpressed. "And who might you be?"

"Ember Rose," I said. "I work for *Vox Populi*."

She gripped my arm. "You work with Alec Hale?" She sighed dreamily. "Tell me how he smells. I imagine a musky scent mixed with fresh pine."

"Um, I can't say I sniff him very often." Though I had been close enough. "I don't think pine is in the mix."

"Rose," she repeated, tapping her chin. "Surely not *the* Rose."

"Hyacinth is my aunt," I said.

She whistled. "Too bad you got saddled with the dark hair. Usually, you can tell a Rose from a mile away."

"I favor my mother, apparently." Black hair, blue eyes, and a host of psychic skills. Thanks, Mom.

"Have you ever considered a tattoo?" she asked, eyeing my exposed skin.

"Not really," I said. "My daughter's not a fan of them."

Desdemona sidled up to me. "What if you told her these tattoos were special?"

"She's ten going on fifty," I said. "She's not going to fall for that."

ANNABEL CHASE

Desdemona hiked up her shirt to reveal a large black dragon tattoo on her back. For a moment it looked like a normal tattoo. Suddenly, the dragon opened its mouth and fire shot across the fairy's back, leaving a tattoo of red flames streaked across her skin.

"Dragon balls of fire," I said. "How does it do that?"

Desdemona pulled down her shirt and faced me. "Fairy magic, of course."

"What happens to the flames?" I asked. "They weren't there originally."

"They fade after a few minutes," she explained. "Until he breathes fire again."

"So what do you think?" Deputy Bolan asked. "Would your daughter approve of a tattoo like that?"

"She might." I tried to decide. "She objects to them because of their permanence, though. She thinks I'll regret what I've done when I'm seventy and it'll hurt like hell to remove it."

Desdemona's brow wrinkled. "Are you sure your daughter is ten?"

"Pretty sure. I was there when she was born," I said.

"So if you're not tattoo shopping, why are you here?" Desdemona asked. "I can't imagine Deputy McSmall and Mighty was eager to see me again after our last run-in."

"We're investigating a curse," Deputy Bolan said. "Some citizens have experienced their worst fears come true."

Desdemona appeared unconcerned. "Sucks to be them. So what does that mean? Some old witch thinks her cat actually *has* eaten off her face?"

I shuddered at the image. "No. There have been a few instances, but the immediate concern is that Alec Hale has succumbed to his vampire tendencies." I deliberately omitted the sheriff's condition.

Desdemona's expression brightened. "He's ruthlessly

114

savaging women with those impressive fangs of his?" She growled. "Come to Mama. Where can I find him?"

"Miss Gilroy, this is serious," Deputy Bolan said. "If you know anything about this, we have to hear the truth. The sheriff can't perform his duties in wolf form." He clapped his hand over his mouth.

"Nice going, Shamrock Sherlock," I grumbled.

"The sheriff is stuck as a wolf? So Starry Hollow is stuck with you as interim sheriff in the meantime?" Desdemona asked. "You're right. You really do need the truth." She leaned forward and parted her lips as though she were about to reveal a hidden secret. "Gotcha." She pulled back and laughed.

I glanced at the deputy, who was fighting the urge to arrest her for being a jerk. "I don't think she knows anything, Deputy."

"She certainly doesn't," he agreed somberly. "Nothing at all."

"Good evening, my darling family," Aunt Hyacinth said. "So pleased we could all be together for dinner."

"And that Uncle Florian isn't a frog," Aspen said.

Aster silenced him with a stern look.

"I can assure you, I'm the most pleased of all about that," Florian replied good-naturedly.

"Is Uncle Granger still a werewolf?" Hudson asked.

Linnea gave an exasperated sigh. "Hudson, we're not supposed to talk about his condition."

"We all know in this house," Aunt Hyacinth said. "But the information goes no further. The Council of Elders is not happy with the situation. The curse has gotten out of hand. They've decided to launch their own investigation."

"What would be your worst nightmare, Grandmother?" Bryn asked.

Aunt Hyacinth contemplated the question. "I think it would be best if I kept it to myself."

"I doubt the ones afflicted so far were running around announcing it to people," Florian said. "The curse must have a way of getting inside the victim's head."

"It's not the curse I'm concerned with," Aunt Hyacinth said.

"Then what?" Florian asked. Understanding flashed in his eyes. "You're worried that one of us would use the information against you at some point? Are you insane, Mother?"

She wiped her mouth with a delicate dab of her napkin. "Simply cautious."

"Simply paranoid is more like it," he replied, and then quickly fell silent.

"Mother, you can't possibly think that one of us would want your worst nightmare to come true," Aster said. "It doesn't say much for how you view your family."

"There's nothing wrong with my view," my aunt said. She took a long sip of her cocktail. Tonight she served one of Linnea's favorites—a Starry Hollow mule. The drinks were served in puckered silver mugs.

"You act like you're the head of a crime family and we're all out to steal your power," Linnea said.

I didn't disagree with her assessment. I couldn't think of a single reason why my aunt would distrust her family members. As far as I knew, the only one who arguably betrayed her was my father and even that was a stretch.

"How is Granger?" Aster asked. "I would imagine it's unpleasant for him being unable to shift."

"Ask Ember," Linnea said. "She's been to see him more than anyone else."

I felt my aunt's steely gaze rest upon me. "Is that so?" she asked.

"I was with him when he turned," I said. "I feel responsible somehow."

"You were with him where?" my aunt asked.

Ugh. Let the interrogation begin.

"In his office," I said. "It wasn't long after Alec went full vampire. I texted the sheriff and he came and tranquilized Alec. I went back to the sheriff's office with him to answer questions about the incident."

Florian gaped at me. "Ember, do you realize you've been present for every single person's nightmare so far?"

A lump formed in my throat. "Yes, Florian. I'm very much aware."

My aunt examined me. "The first one took place during the board meeting, where we were all present."

"That's right," I said. "And then Bentley, Trupti, Alec, and the sheriff."

Aster frowned. "Can that be a coincidence, Mother?"

"I'm not sure what to make of it," my aunt replied, swirling the liquid in her glass. "What does Deputy Bolan think?"

"We've spoken to a couple of suspects, but no solid leads have turned up," I said. "And Wren doesn't think it can be me. He said I'd know. That I'd feel something." But I felt nothing except guilty.

"I agree," Aunt Hyacinth said. "If it can overtake the sheriff and Alec Hale, the curse is too powerful for you to have a hand in it."

"Maybe someone should make Florian's worst fear come true," Aster said. "At least he'd end up with a job or married to a reputable witch."

Florian pretended to laugh. "Such a quirky sense of humor, dear sister."

"Isn't Florian working at the tourism office?" I asked.

"He comes and goes," Aster said airily. "I haven't seen *you* there recently."

I straightened in my chair. "I've been preoccupied with hexing and cursing the townsfolk, apparently. I'll come this week. I swear."

"Ember's been given an extra coven session with Wren," Aunt Hyacinth said. "Ember is a Rose and magic comes first for this family. Everything else is secondary."

At the mention of family, my gaze shifted to the banner with the family crest above the mantel, with its dark blue background, full moon, and stars with a red rose in front of the moon. The family motto—*carpe noctem*—was embroidered along the bottom. Seize the night. What if everyone was wrong about me? What if the magic inside me was taking the motto too literally and dragging people's nightmares into the light of day? And, if that was the case, how would I stop it?

CHAPTER 13

I STOOD in the kitchen with my wand pointed at the crock-pot. I figured I'd try to practice magic and cooking at the same time. If Linnea could touch the oven and create a pot roast, I could work wonders with a crockpot. Marley would be so impressed. I thumbed through the magical recipe book with my free hand, trying to find the page I'd just lost. I was fascinated to learn how meatloaf could be made via magic.

PP3 sat by my feet, as though expecting pieces of food to drop on the floor. He didn't seem to realize I hadn't started yet.

A sudden yelp made me jump. For a second, I thought I'd accidentally stepped on his paw. It happened on occasion, usually when he was shadowing me in a narrow space like the kitchen.

"What is it, buddy?" I asked. He cowered beside me, so I bent to examine him.

A knock on the door interrupted my inspection. PP3 didn't bark at the intrusion. Instead, he remained rooted to the kitchen floor.

"I'll be right back," I told him, and went to answer the door.

I was shocked to see my aunt on the doorstep. She usually sent Simon to deliver messages or to escort me back to the main house.

"Good day, niece," she said. "May I come in?" Today's kaftan was covered in a design of pink and red roses. At least there were no cat faces to upset PP3, although now I understood his odd behavior a moment ago. My aunt intimidated him even through walls and doors.

I stepped aside. "My cottage is your cottage."

Once inside, she stopped and surveyed the homey interior. "I suppose you've done what you can with the place under the circumstances."

I followed her gaze. Done what I can? The cottage was ready for the pages of *Adorable Homes Interior* or whatever magazine existed for the purpose of showing off warm, inviting spaces.

"Aren't you going to offer me a drink or a bite to eat?" Aunt Hyacinth asked.

"I wasn't sure you planned to stay that long," I replied.

"Doesn't matter what my intentions are, darling. You should always ask."

Ugh. My aunt and her acute sense of propriety.

"Would you like a drink, Aunt Hyacinth?" I asked through clenched teeth.

"That's better." She paused. "No, thank you. It's early and I suspect you've been lured into buying the cheap stuff. I should send Simon shopping for you one day. He has exceptional taste."

I held my breath so as not to give her a severe tongue lashing. After all, she was the person I had to thank for my life now. It was Aunt Hyacinth's concern that brought

Marley and me to Starry Hollow. I could forgive a lot when my daughter was as happy as Marley was now.

"What brings you all the way across the grass?" I asked. "Is Simon injured?"

I could tell by the pinched look on my aunt's face that she didn't want to say whatever words were about to leave her coral-colored lips.

"Ember, your presence has been requested before the Council of Elders," she said.

"Again? Why?" I'd attended a meeting once before when I first arrived in town and the council wanted to interrogate me. I didn't care to repeat the process.

"They wish to speak with you about the nightmare curse. I told you they'd launched their own investigation. They're very concerned."

Inwardly, I groaned. "And they think I'm to blame?"

"Not necessarily, but, as you mentioned at dinner, you do seem to be the common thread."

Me and my big mouth. When would I learn? "You said yourself that you don't believe I had anything to do with it." And I desperately wanted to believe her.

"I still don't, darling. You're not that capable."

"Um, thanks." I blew out a breath. "So, when do I need to make an appearance?"

"This evening," my aunt replied. "I'll already be at the meeting, but I'll send transport."

"You mean a horse."

"Yes, of course. The horse will know the way."

"What about...?"

"I'll send Mrs. Babcock to look after Marley as well," she said, anticipating my question. She paused for a beat. "I don't know where you learned it, Ember, but you're a good mother."

"Is it possible for you to say anything nice without it sounding like a backhanded compliment?" I asked.

She considered the question. "You should simply say thank you."

"Thanks," I muttered.

I caught sight of PP3 in the kitchen doorway, wary of taking a closer step.

"Why is my dog so afraid of you?" I asked.

"Because he's intelligent," she said, and then added, "for a dog." She moved toward the door. "The horse will be out front at nine o'clock. Don't be late."

"No pumpkin carriage?" I queried.

My aunt ignored me and sailed out the door.

I wasn't late. Mrs. Babcock made sure of that. She arrived early with a knitting bag because Marley was already tucked in bed. Council meeting or not, it was a school night and I wasn't going to disrupt my daughter's sleep pattern.

"They can be a fierce lot, but don't let them intimidate you," Mrs. Babcock warned, as I prepared to leave the cottage.

"It's hard not to be, with all their cloaks and candles," I said.

"They've been around a long time and they think they own this town, but they don't," she said firmly.

"No, they can't own this town because Aunt Hyacinth already does."

Mrs. Babcock smiled. "She is rather powerful, your aunt. You stay on her good side and you'll be right as rain."

"I try," I said, "but she doesn't make it easy sometimes."

"She can be difficult, but she loves her family. Make no mistake about it. That's her saving grace."

"She spoils Florian," I said. "That's not good for either one of them."

"And you spoil Marley in your own way," Mrs. Babcock said. "Yet no one is telling you how to be a better parent."

"Marley's ten," I said. "Florian is a grown man."

"But he'll always be your aunt's baby boy. Doesn't matter how old he is." Her eyes twinkled. "You'll see when Marley gets older. It'll be exactly the same for you."

PP3 began to bark—a signal that my horse had arrived.

"Hopefully, I won't be late getting back," I said.

Mrs. Babcock settled into a chair with her knitting bag. "Don't hurry on my account. I'm something of a night owl."

I slipped on my silver cloak, tucked my wand in the pocket, and headed out the door. The large white horse stood on the front lawn, practically glowing in the darkness.

"Hey there, Candle," I said.

The horse whinnied in response.

I stroked the soft mane. "I guess I need to get myself up here this time." I wasn't the most adept at getting myself on the back of a horse, not without my cousins to help me.

It wasn't easy and it took a few embarrassing tries, but I finally managed. Candle was kind enough to lower herself so I could get a solid grip before throwing a leg over the side. Very dignified. Good thing I was wearing pants under my cloak.

The moon was high in the sky and the stars blinked in greeting as we traveled along the coastline toward the hidden cave where council meetings were held. I listened to the sound of the waves as they crashed against the rocks and then flattened into silence.

"You're a good driver," I said to the horse.

We stopped outside the mouth of the cave and Candle maneuvered close to a boulder, so that I didn't have to drop all the way to the ground.

"Clever Candle," I said, patting her back. "Now wait here in case we need to make a fast getaway. Who knows what crimes the Council of Old Timers will accuse me of?"

I sauntered into the cave, not as intimidated as the last time I was here. At least this time I knew what to expect. My aunt met me in the neck of the cave.

"Good work, my dear," she said. "Punctuality is a virtue. Never forget it."

"Hard to forget when there's a big white horse outside your front door."

"Try not to answer questions that haven't been asked," she whispered. "Let the council do the work."

In other words, keep your big mouth shut. Got it.

We entered the larger part of the cave where the council members sat around a table.

"Our special guest has arrived," Aunt Hyacinth announced. "Ember, please take a seat beside me."

I joined my aunt at the table and managed a smile. "Good evening, everyone. Haven't seen most of you since the last time I was summoned here to defend myself against criminal charges."

My aunt shot me a disapproving look.

"I understand you were with Alec Hale when he was overtaken by the curse," Victorine said. Victorine Del Bianco was the head of the vampire coven.

"I was," I said. "He came into the office when I was there alone and began to act strangely."

"I don't like the way people are talking about him," Victorine said. "Using phrases like 'going full vamp.' It's disrespectful to our community."

I didn't know how to respond. "I've been to see him at the sheriff's office. He asked me to stop visiting until he's back to…" I nearly said 'normal' but wondered whether Victorine would object to that term as well. "Back to his old self."

"I've been to see him for myself," Victorine said. "He looks unwell in my opinion. I hired a warlock to try and reverse the spell, but it had no effect."

My aunt slowly turned to stare down Victorine. "You did what?"

The vampire rolled her eyes. "Yes, yes. I know the coven is not a fan of warlocks."

"Why would you do such a thing?" asked Oliver Dagwood, an elderly wizard.

"Because Alec is one of mine and it's my duty to take care of him," Victorine said. "I expect the pack has taken similar steps to reverse the spell on Sheriff Nash." She eyed the elderly werewolf, Arthur Rutledge.

Arthur hung his head. "We have, indeed, but to no avail. The pack is greatly concerned about the sheriff's worsening condition. His body isn't coping well with his lupine form. He needs to shift."

"So I take it you didn't call me out here to witness your disagreements," I interjected.

The head of every council member turned toward me.

"True. We did not," Misty Brookline said. The fairy gave me a pointed look. "We have been discussing the various nightmares at length and have determined that the only commonality is you, Miss Rose."

"Yes, I came to that conclusion myself, but as my aunt so wisely stated, I'm not nearly advanced enough with magic to perform a curse like this. I wouldn't even know where to begin."

"She only recently selected her starter wand," Aunt Hyacinth added. "She's mastered locking and unlocking recently. That's it. She's hardly setting the paranormal world on fire."

I cast a sidelong glance at my aunt. I thought I was a natural and now she was underplaying my skills. She also seemed to be keeping very careful tabs on my progress. Why was it so important to her? Because I was a Rose…or some other reason?

"Walk us through each curse as it happened," Victorine said. "Starting with the first one."

"I was present for the first one," Aunt Hyacinth said. "I told you that."

"Let the girl tell us from her perspective," Victorine said. "We're well acquainted with your perspective on all matters, Hyacinth."

My aunt's eyes glinted in the candlelight. Her expression said that she did not take kindly to the vampire's dismissive tone of voice. I didn't mind being called 'girl,' though. Even though I knew it was disrespectful, it made me feel young.

I relayed each curse as it unfolded, giving every detail I remembered about the victims and their reactions. When I finished, everyone stared at me silently.

"No big ideas?" I asked. "Come on. You're supposed to be a bunch of wise elders with your fancy staffs and your cave-dwelling meetings."

My aunt placed a hand on my arm. "Thank you for your contribution, Ember."

"I have a question for Ember," Arthur said. "Why were you alone with Sheriff Nash in his office?"

"We were talking about Alec," I said.

"Is that all you were doing?" Arthur pressed.

I squirmed in my seat. I didn't want to reveal that he'd been drinking on the job. I knew they would misunderstand and my aunt was always looking for a reason to cast aspersions on the sheriff's character. She wasn't a fan of werewolves.

"And what about Alec?" Victorine asked. "Why were you alone with him in the office? Where was Tanya?"

"Tanya was out and Bentley had just left," I said.

I didn't like the direction the questions were going. They felt accusatory, as though I maneuvered to be alone with the victims.

"I wasn't alone with Bentley when his fear took hold," I said. "It was an art gallery full of people. And, I told you, the board meeting included my family."

"But you were alone with Trupti," Victorine said. "She also told me that you and Alec seem to have developed a… special relationship."

I gulped. I felt my aunt's eyes burning a whole through my skin. "He's my boss. I guess you can call that special."

"That's not what she meant, I assure you," Victorine said. "Perhaps you were unhappy when you discovered his previous relationship with Trupti and decided to punish them both."

My eyes popped. "Are you nuts? First of all, I told you my magic sucks at this point. Second of all, I'm not stupid enough to mess with two powerful vampires. Bentley, sure, he's an elf and not very scary, but Alec…" I trailed off. "And Sheriff Nash is a werewolf. He could have killed me if Deputy Bolan hadn't come along with a tranquilizer gun."

"Score one for the leprechauns," Mervin O'Malley blurted. His cheeks burned crimson.

"I'll be honest," I said. "Deputy Bolan isn't my favorite Starry Hollow resident, but he's good at his job."

Mervin smiled proudly. "That he is. And people were skeptical when the sheriff announced him as the new deputy." He looked around the room. "Some of *you* were skeptical, as I recall."

"Now can we stop wasting time on my niece and focus on identifying the real culprit?" Aunt Hyacinth asked. "The curses are going to keep happening unless we get to the bottom of it."

"I think it might make sense to broaden the scope of the

investigation," I said. "Talk to residents who may have a chip on their shoulder. Paranormals mad at the world, not revenge on a specific target."

"That might explain the absence of a connection between the victims," Oliver said.

"So you think someone is expressing anger or frustration through random acts of magical violence?" Arthur queried.

"It's a possibility," I said. "Everyone else I've talked to so far has been ruled out. We need to switch gears."

Misty raised a hand. "Don't you find it odd that there hasn't been a new curse since Alec and Sheriff Nash were afflicted?"

"Why is that odd?" Oliver asked.

"Because they'd been happening one after the other and now there's a lull," the older fairy said. "Why? Maybe if we can figure out the reason, we can catch the culprit."

It was a good question. "And some of the nightmares came and went quickly," I added, "but Alec and the sheriff are still under the spell. Why?"

The council members began to murmur to each other. It was always disconcerting when not even the oldest and wisest among us had an answer. Memories of Alec's tortured face and the sheriff's painful transformation sprang to mind and my stomach twisted.

"Perhaps because they are the strongest of the afflicted group," Amaryllis Elderflower said.

"Then the curse should be shorter, not longer," Oliver pointed out.

My aunt placed her palms flat on the table. "We can come up with theories all night. Before we do so, I hereby move to end the speculation regarding my niece and allow her to leave. Are we clear?"

"I second the motion," Amaryllis said.

Heads bobbed up and down.

My aunt nodded to me. "You're free to go, my dear. Candle will get you home safely."

"Thank you," I said, to no one in particular. "I'm sorry it wasn't me. In some ways, that would make all this easier. Then we could reverse it."

"My word, Ember." My aunt's expression softened. "Be careful, darling. I do believe your heart is showing."

CHAPTER 14

I WAS SO BLINDED by clumps of hair in my face that I failed to notice I was being followed. Candle noticed first—her nostrils flared and she began to pick up speed along the coastal path.

"Slow down, girl," I said. "What's wrong?"

She whinnied in response.

"Is there a spell that lets me speak horse?" I asked.

A low growl reverberated behind me and I knew what was spooking the majestic horse. I craned my neck and saw several sets of yellow eyes glowing in the inky black of night.

"Crap on a stick. Werewolves," I whispered. Were they like the sheriff, trapped in wolf form and slowly going nuts? Or just garden-variety werewolves out for a midnight run?

I gripped Candle tightly, uncertain what to do. Were they growling at the horse or me? Maybe we were in their way. I guided the horse to the side, my heart thumping wildly, hoping the pack would simply pass by.

They didn't.

My hand slipped into the pocket of the cloak and my fingers curled around the base of the wand. Werewolves weren't doors, so the locking spell was useless, but I figured I'd come up with something in a pinch.

The wolves circled around the horse. They clearly had no intention of passing by.

"What do you want?" I asked, in the voice I used to reserve for unsolicited sales calls at my apartment.

The wolf in the front bared its fangs and my skin tingled with fear.

"Sheriff Nash is my friend," I yelled. "He wouldn't like whatever it is you're trying to do to me." I brandished my wand like a sword. "I have magic and I'm not afraid to use it."

The growls deepened and the wolves crept closer. The nearest one looked ready to lunge forward. I ran through different spells in my head to see if there was anything to save me from a wolf attack.

I pointed my wand and said the first spell that came to mind. "*Mutatio purpureus.*"

Even in the darkness, I could see that all the wolves' fur coats turned purple. Uh oh. Not the defensive spell I was hoping for.

The wolf in the front began to shift. Bones popped and muscles stretched until a fully naked man stood in front of me. His hair—all his hair—was bright purple.

"What in hell's bells?" he asked, raking a hand through his colorful mop.

"Who are you and why are you following me?" I demanded, pointing my wand in the most menacing fashion I could manage.

"The name's Lucas Black. We want to know what you did to the sheriff," he said. "We know he's sick and that you're responsible."

"I'm not responsible," I insisted. "In fact, I was just cleared by the Council of Elders. Your leader was there. Ask Arthur."

Lucas seemed surprised by this news. "Wyatt said you're the one thing that connects all the victims."

"Wyatt said that?" Anger boiled within me. "It's true I was with each of the victims, but I didn't curse them. I wouldn't even know how. Besides, I like everyone involved. I have no reason to harm them." I kept Bentley's annoying habits to myself. Now didn't seem like the time to mention his penchant for coughing without covering his mouth.

"I've been to visit the sheriff as often as I can because I'm worried about him," I said. "I don't want anything bad to happen to him. He's been one of the bright spots…" I stopped when I realized I was saying too much. Members of the pack didn't need to know my personal feelings about Sheriff Nash. I hadn't even admitted them to myself.

Lucas grinned. "So you like the sheriff?"

Another wolf shifted to a nude woman with cropped purple hair. "You mean you kinda like him, or you *like* him?"

"Are we in third grade?" I asked, trying not to stare at the woman's enormous boobs. How did she keep her balance? Okay, maybe we were in third grade.

Another naked man popped up where a wolf had been crouched. "I think she really likes him. I heard they had sex in his office and that's what turned him into a wolf."

My eyes bulged. "Sweet baby Elvis. That is *not* what happened. Who told you that?"

"Someone on the forensics team," the werewolf replied.

"That's…that's crazy," I sputtered. "I have not had sex with the sheriff. I haven't even kissed him."

"But you want to," the woman said. "Because you *like* him."

"Okay, listen up," I said. "It's late. I'm tired and I want to go home. I didn't curse your favorite sheriff with my magical hoo-ha, and the extent to which I like him is my business, not yours. Got it?"

The werewolves looked at each other and shrugged.

"Can you change our hair back to its normal color first?" Lucas asked. "I don't want to get laughed out of the bar tonight."

"Not me," the woman said. "I kinda like the eggplant color."

"Sorry. I'm not doing individual spells," I told her. I pointed my wand and used *rescindo to* restore their natural colors.

"If we find out you've lied to us about the sheriff," Lucas said, "we'll be back."

"You can come back," I said, "but I won't be here. I don't make a habit of hanging out in the middle of the forest at night, unlike you guys."

With those words, I nudged Candle to take me home. She galloped down the path, leaving the wolves far behind. It was only when we arrived back at the cottage that I realized my hands were shaking.

I was exhausted the next morning when I dragged myself down to the *Vox Populi* office. I located Tanya and Bentley in Alec's office, lamenting his absence.

"This is worse than when he was a frog," Tanya moaned.

"Of course it is," Bentley said. "When he was a frog, he had those adorable little fangs. In crazed vampire mode, his fangs are downright scary."

"His little frog fangs were cute," I said. I tried to forget the fact that he'd spent time in my bedroom in his frog form and had seen me naked. "Has he ever gone feral vamp before?" Maybe his condition was unrelated to the sheriff's. A coincidence.

Tanya vehemently shook her head. "Absolutely not. Alec Hale is a true gentleman."

"Yes, that's been my impression," I said, "but I haven't known him very long. I was wondering if he'd gone through a bad boy vampire phase before he discovered a love of tailored suits and shiny loafers."

"He's much older than I am," Tanya said. "I'll be the first to admit, I don't know much about his history. He doesn't speak of it often."

"I think it's why he writes fantasy books," Bentley said. "As a way of dealing with his past."

"A coping mechanism?" I asked. Some people drank; Alec wrote bestselling novels as a way of exorcising his demons, except that, technically, he *was* a demon.

"You've only read *The Final Prophecy*," Bentley said. "If you read some of the others, you'll understand what I mean."

Now I was curious. "That reminds me…The dedication in *The Final Prophecy* is to someone called Tatiana. Who is she?" Marley had noticed the dedication page that I'd skipped over and asked me about it.

"I think I'd rather keep what I know to myself," Tanya said, and began tidying papers on Alec's desk.

"Tanya, you're just moving papers around," I accused. "Tell me what you know about Tatiana. Is she the one who left town with a centaur a few years ago? The woman he and Sheriff Nash were both in love with?"

Bentley raised a skinny elfin eyebrow. "Who told you that?"

"Linnea," I said. "Wyatt used to tell her everything going on with his brother when they were married."

"Too bad Wyatt didn't tell her everything going on with *him*," Bentley said. "Could have saved your cousin a lot of heartache."

"We're not talking about Linnea," I said. "We're talking about the mysterious Tatiana."

"Go on, Tanya," Bentley urged. "Tell her."

I glanced from Bentley to Tanya. "You're hiding something. I can feel it."

Tanya placed her fingertips on the desk and inhaled sharply. "Tatiana is my niece."

"Your niece?" I echoed. "She's a fairy?"

Tanya nodded slowly. "I feel somewhat responsible for the whole debacle, to be honest. I'm the one who introduced her to Alec, you see."

"That's not the whole story," Bentley said. "Don't blame yourself for any of it, Tanya. You know perfectly well that Tatiana had fairy magic at her disposal."

"Don't all fairies have fairy magic at their disposal?" I asked. "Except ex-convicts." Fairies like Robina Mapperton, the new owner of Snips-n-Clips, were stripped of their fairy magic when convicted of serious crimes.

"Bentley means she used fairy magic in an unethical manner," Tanya said. "She liked Alec, but she liked the idea of watching him compete for her more. She pitted the sheriff and Alec against each other as a game." Tanya pressed her lips together. "I'm not proud of her behavior. It was the best-case scenario when she left town."

I wrinkled my brow. "Do they know she used magic on them?"

"They do," Tanya said. "And I think they were both humiliated by the experience."

"Then why do they still hate each other?" I asked. "If neither one of them was actually in love with her?"

"But they *believed* they were," Bentley said. "The emotions they experienced felt genuine. The love, the jealousy, the ultimate humiliation. Don't discount the power of magic."

"That's awful," I said. "Do you keep in touch with Tatiana?"

Tanya's expression darkened. "I do not, although my sister updates me on occasion. I suffer the information in silence. And should she ever flutter a wing back in Starry Hollow, I'll be the first to see about having her passport revoked."

"What about the centaur?" I asked. "Is she still with him?"

"No, she tired of him rather quickly," Tanya said. "The last I heard, she was in Asia with yet another paranormal paramour."

"It's hard to imagine Sheriff Nash or Alec being taken advantage of by a fairy," I said. "They both seem too smart for that."

"Tatiana is a gifted fairy," Tanya said, with the hint of a smile. "Runs in the family."

"But you chose the light and she chose darkness," Bentley said.

"I don't think she chose it, so much as it chose her," Tanya said. "She was a troublemaker from the first, I'm afraid. I never should have introduced her to Alec."

I patted Tanya's shoulder. "This happened years ago and both men seem unaffected, except for the fact that they loathe each other. That was bound to happen anyway with the whole werewolf versus vampire thing."

"You're very sweet, Ember," Tanya said. "I appreciate it." She fixed her concerned gaze on me. "It's you I'm worried about now."

"What do you mean?" I asked.

She cleared her throat. "Well, it seems both gentlemen have shown a preference for you."

"A preference for me? Are we in a Jane Austen novel?" Because I'd be totally cool with that, despite the silly bonnets.

"They both like you," Bentley blurted. "There, I said it. By the gods, it's like watching a wildlife documentary on mating rituals. Now can we stop pretending we don't notice?" He shot Tanya an accusatory look.

I hesitated. I didn't want to admit the things Alec had said to me. They were far too personal. Instead, I said, "The sheriff doesn't like me in that way. It's more in the vein of a tagalong little sister."

"If Sheriff Nash looked at my sister the way he looks at you, I'd be locking her up for the next five years," Bentley said.

"Okay, first of all, that's sexist. Why should your sister be locked up because a man finds her attractive? Second of all, you have a sister? How did I not know this?" And here I thought Bentley was the annoying brother I never had. I didn't realize the position was already taken. I felt a little disappointed.

"His sister's name is Eloise and she lives in Elf Haven," Tanya said. "She attends the university there."

"Is she a journalism major?" I asked.

"Magical engineering," Bentley said. "She loves to tinker."

"Good for her," I said. Inwardly, I sighed with relief that I was able to shift the conversation away from me. I had a big mouth at the best of times, and I didn't want to blab to Alec's employees that he had the hots for me, especially now when he was in such a vulnerable state.

"Have you and Deputy Bolan come up with any new leads?" Bentley asked. "The curse seems to be getting worse with each new victim."

"I met with the Council of Elders last night," I said. "It's likely we want to cast a wider net. Instead of focusing on the specific victims, try to think of residents that have suffered a loss recently. Magic users that might be angry at the world and wreaking havoc out of anger or frustration."

"That's an interesting thought," Tanya said. "I do know a rather horrible story."

"And we didn't run a story on it?" Bentley asked, annoyed.

Tanya shook her head. "Not that kind of story. Her name is Daffodil. I know her from the farmer's market." The fairy looked at me. "She's one of yours. You might want to speak with her." She clucked her tongue. "Tragic story involving her familiar."

"I'll head over in a few minutes," I said.

"I should get a move on, too, if I expect to visit Alec before my hair appointment," Tanya said. "I'm going to stop by the blood bank on my way to the sheriff's office and pick him up a nice, thick bloodshake."

"That sounds…gross," I said. "But I guess he'll love it."

"I do hope he snaps out of it soon," Tanya said. "The paper needs him."

"Plus, he has a book deadline," Bentley said. "I saw it on his calendar."

Tanya snapped her fingers. "You're right. I'll need to keep an eye on that."

"Which book is he working on?" I asked. "Another one in *The Final Prophecy* series?"

"Not sure," Tanya said. "He's been very secretive with this one."

"Typical Alec," I said. "Skulking around writing secret books."

"I'm going to finish the article I'm writing," Bentley said. "*Someone* needs to keep this paper going during our fearless leader's incarceration."

"How's Meadow, by the way?" I asked. "Did everything get resolved between you two lovebirds?"

He lifted his chin a fraction. "It did, actually. I'm taking her to dinner tonight."

"I'm glad."

He opened his mouth, as though ready for a snappy comeback. "You are?"

"Of course I am. I don't like seeing you miserable, Bentley. It brings down the whole vibe in the office."

"So my happiness is really about your comfort level."

I folded my arms. "Would you rather I mock you mercilessly? Because I can pivot with the best of them."

Bentley waved me off. "Thank you for your warm tidings." He slipped back to his desk before I could say more.

I lingered in Alec's office, wishing there was something I could do to help him. I sat behind his desk and tapped on his keyboard. Maybe if I could find his book information, I could let the publisher know that he'd be late.

The screen lit up and I scanned the file directory for the most recent saves. I clicked on the file labeled A.B. Ellis. Maybe that was his contact at the publisher's office.

The file opened and I read the first page that included a title and summary of the book. *Filthy Witch* by A.B. Ellis. My jaw dropped as I continued to read. The book was about a forbidden romance between a centuries-old vampire and a new witch. I fanned myself as I read the remainder of the description. I had no doubt that A.B. Ellis was Alec's pen name. He could disguise his identity, but he couldn't disguise his voice. I recognized it easily after reading *The Final Prophecy*.

"Alec, you naughty vampire," I said. Resisting the temptation to read more, I closed the file. According to his calendar, the deadline was still two weeks from now. He had to be better before then. He just had to.

Bentley poked his head in the doorway. "Didn't you say you were driving out to see Daffodil?"

I shut down the computer before Bentley came over to see what I was doing. "Yes, yes. I'm going now. Don't rush me."

He gave me a curious look before disappearing back to his desk. I tried to block the book's description from my mind. Alec was already deadly attractive. The last thing I needed was a steamy romance novel that featured the two of us as its main characters.

I blew out a sexually frustrated breath and left the office.

Daffodil lived on a burstberry farm on the northwestern outskirts of town. The white farmhouse had a gabled roof and a generous front porch complete with two red rocking chairs. The setting was as picturesque as the house itself. Fields stretched away from the house in every direction—an oasis of calm.

Daffodil appeared on the horizon in a wide-brimmed hat and gardening gloves. White hair poked out from beneath the hat. She didn't smile when she spotted me in the driveway.

"Are you lost?" Daffodil removed her gloves and tucked them into the back of her waistband.

"Not today. This is quite a place you have here," I said. "I've only seen farmhouses like this on television."

Daffodil surveyed the tranquil location. "It has its charms. Do you like burstberries?"

"What's not to like?"

"I grow twenty different varieties here," she said.

I balked. "There are twenty different varieties of one berry?"

This time she smiled. "More than that. I only grow twenty here. Some varieties are newer than others. My family started with Heartland and Jubilee years ago and expanded from there."

"Sounds like a lot of work," I said.

"It is. We pick the berries by hand."

My brow lifted. "You don't even use magic?"

Daffodil laughed. "Of course we use magic. We're not complete heathens."

"Do you distribute locally?" I asked, remembering Tanya's mention of the farmer's market.

"We serve all the paranormal towns in the southeastern United States," she said proudly. "But I get the feeling you didn't come here to talk to me about my berries." She fanned herself with her hat. "Where are my manners? Can I get you a refreshment? Come sit on the porch where it's cooler."

I followed her onto the welcoming porch and sat in one of the red rocking chairs.

"How about a burstberry lemonade?" she asked. She dropped her hat on the porch and wiped her brow.

"Sounds great."

Daffodil disappeared into the house and returned a minute later with two glasses. I took a curious sip. I had no idea what to expect.

"This is delicious," I said.

"Thank you. It's a family recipe passed down from generation to generation." She sat in the adjacent rocking chair. "Now I know why you look familiar. I saw you at the last coven meeting. You're the Rose witch."

"Ember."

"And how are you finding life in Starry Hollow so far, Ember?"

"Never a dull moment," I admitted.

She began to rock gently and sipped her drink. "I understand you have a daughter."

"Yes, Marley. She's ten."

Daffodil lit up. "How exciting. She'll come into her magic next year."

"Hopefully. She's very excited. Do you have any children?"

Her expression clouded over. "Afraid not. Would have loved a few witches and wizards running rampant around the farm, but our wondrous goddess had other plans."

"Are you married?"

"No." She gave me a sad smile. "The absence of a wizard in my life was a major part of the problem."

"That blows."

"You lost a husband, if I recall correctly. That blows, too."

I nodded. "An accident. He was a truck driver."

"A shame. Your parents. Your husband. All gone. So much tragedy in the world. Makes you wonder why we bother."

"Bother with what?"

She shrugged. "Anything at all. Some days it's not worth putting on your cloak."

"Did you know my parents?"

"I did, as a matter of fact." She sucked down the remainder of her drink and set the empty glass on the floorboard beside the chair. "Wonderful people. Deserved better."

"I find that a lot."

"What's that?"

"That people deserve better than they get," I said.

"You're far too young for that attitude. So, how can I help you, Ember? I imagine you didn't come here to discuss the world's ills, as pleasurable as that is."

"I'm writing an article for *Vox Populi* about some recent activities in town."

She frowned. "What kind of activities?"

"People's worst fears coming true," I said.

"Why would I know anything about that?"

I hesitated. "I understand one of your worst fears came true recently. I'd like to know whether it's related."

Daffodil's lips formed a thin line. "I take it you mean Miss Tiddlywinks."

Her cat was named Miss Tiddlywinks? "Your familiar," I said. "I've been told she met a tragic end."

Daffodil's eyes brimmed with tears. "Indeed, she did. I'm still recovering, not that I'll ever fully recover from it. She was my world. My closest companion."

"Would you mind telling me what happened, if it's not too difficult?"

Daffodil struggled to speak. "We...we were out in the field like normal. Miss T always accompanied me on my daily chores. We had the best chats." She paused, remembering.

"Your familiar spoke to you?" I asked.

"Telepathically," she said. "Do you have a familiar yet, Ember?"

"No. I have a dog. A Yorkshire terrier." And PP3 was definitely not my familiar. There were some days I wasn't even sure he recognized me.

"A dog," she repeated. "How interesting. Does he speak to you?"

"Only through the power of whining and barking."

"I hope one day you'll be as lucky as me," Daffodil said. "Miss T put all other familiars to shame."

"Was she ill?" I asked.

"No. In some ways, that may have been better." She cleared her throat. "We were out in the field and I noticed three birds of prey flying overhead."

"Is that unusual?"

She shook her white head. "Not really. We get a lot of small rodents in the fields that attract them. We had one incident a few years ago where a bird chased Miss T, but she managed to escape into the house."

The hairs on the back of my neck prickled. "But not this time?"

Daffodil closed her eyes in an effort to collect herself. "It was so unexpected. I don't know why they came for her, especially when I was present. I didn't have my wand handy, not that there was time to react. It all happened so quickly."

"One of the birds took her?" I asked.

Daffodil nodded, fighting tears. "Picked her up in its beak by the scruff of her neck and flew off with the other two birds flanking it." Her hand flew to cover her mouth as she began to sob.

"I'm really sorry, Daffodil," I said. "That's awful. Did you ever find her?"

She nodded. "I buried her on the farm. Then I began keeping my wand on me at all times. Last week the birds made another appearance. I killed all three of them, then I cooked them and ate them."

"You...ate them?"

"Even their hearts," she said, wearing a satisfied expression. "That's called vanquishing an enemy."

I sat perfectly still, momentarily stunned into silence. I made a mental note never to mess with Daffodil. She was tougher than her name suggested.

"How have you been coping since Miss T died?"

"I was a wreck until I got my revenge," she said. "I've felt a little better every day since then."

"I guess this was your worst nightmare come true," I said. A definite motive for wanting others to experience the same heartbreak.

Her answer surprised me. "No, it certainly wasn't."

"Why not?" What could be worse?

"Because my worst fear didn't involve my familiar being carried off by a bird of prey," she replied.

"Did it involve the death of Miss T in any capacity?"

She shook her head. "It was the opposite, in fact. If something happened to me before Miss T, I didn't want her to be left alone. We had such a strong connection." She hesitated. "I also had the irrational fear that she would eat off my face if no one discovered my body quickly enough."

"That's understandable," I said, inwardly cringing.

"I hated the thought of leaving her behind," Daffodil said. "I had a recurring dream where she was alone in the farmhouse, crying for me. Not understanding where I'd gone. I never wanted her to think I abandoned her."

Observing Daffodil now, there was no way she was responsible for the nightmare curse. Her grief and pain were focused inward, not outward.

"I doubt she would have thought that," I said. "She knew how much you loved her."

She hugged herself. "I guess I don't have to worry about that nightmare anymore."

Her comment sparked an idea. "You must know Montague. He's a wizard—the one that lost his wife seven years ago."

Daffodil nodded vaguely. "Yes, of course. I haven't seen him in years, though."

"No surprise there. He tends to stick to his house unless he's…" I nearly said *drunk*. "Unless he's in the mood to be social."

"Are you trying to set me up on a date? Because that broomstick has flown."

"Not a date," I said. "Although I disagree that it's too late for you. You're in great shape and you clearly would like companionship."

"The farmhouse does get lonely sometimes," she admitted.

"Montague's wife had a familiar called Libby. She's very sweet. I think she'd be happier in a place like this. Montague's been too caught up in his own grief to properly care for Libby. She needs love and affection."

Daffodil looked thoughtful. "Do you think he'd give her up? After all, it's his last earthly connection to his wife."

"I think he feels guilty for not taking care of her, but also guilty because he thinks giving up Libby means giving up his wife. If you took in the cat, I think that might help Montague finally move on."

"I would be willing to meet Libby," the older witch said. "I think we should see if we get along before I commit to a new roommate."

"I agree one hundred percent," I said. "I'll speak to Montague and see when might be a good time for you to stop by. I hope it works out." It would be nice for something positive to come out of all this.

"Thank you, Ember," she said. "So do I."

CHAPTER 15

L<small>INNEA</small> finally convinced Wyatt to pay his brother a visit. She didn't want to accompany him for fear that he'd read too much into it, so I agreed to go in her place and make sure Wyatt behaved himself.

"Brother, what big teeth you have," Wyatt said. He kneeled, peering through the cell door at the sequestered wolf.

"You're taunting him?" I asked. "Is that smart?"

Wyatt shrugged. "No one ever accused me of being smart." He fixed his attention on his brother. "How're you holding up in there, Granger?"

The wolf lowered his head.

"I hate to say it, but I'm glad it's you in there and not me," Wyatt said. "Then again, we both know I love our true nature. My nightmare would be something else entirely."

The wolf cocked his head, as though interested to hear more.

"Oh, you know perfectly well, brother," Wyatt said. "Don't give me those puppy eyes." He heaved a sigh. "We both know it would be seeing Linnea in love with someone else."

I stood by in silence.

"How long do you think he'll be stuck like this?" Wyatt asked. "When will the blasted curse wear off?"

"We don't know," I said. "It wore off quickly for the others. It's weird that it's lasting longer for Alec and your brother."

"They must've pissed off the wrong witch," Wyatt said, turning back to the wolf. "Maybe a bad date, brother?"

"I don't think they pissed off anyone in particular," I said. "It seems to be more random than that." I didn't bother scolding him for telling the pack it was my fault.

"What's the coven doing about this?" Wyatt asked, whirling on me. "This has to be the work of a witch or wizard."

My eyes widened. "Not necessarily. Besides, how would I know what the coven decides at the top level? I'm not exactly in charge."

"You're a Rose," he said simply.

Deputy Bolan came into the room with a tray of raw meat. "Dinner for the sheriff."

Wyatt sniffed the food as it passed by. "Smells good."

My stomach turned at the sight of it. "Yummy."

The deputy used a pair of tongs to drop the slab of meat through the barred window. "Sorry about the lack of presentation, Sheriff."

The wolf sniffed the meat before turning away. He dropped down onto his belly and rested his head on his front paws.

"That's odd," Wyatt said. He shot the deputy a quizzical look. "Why isn't he eating?"

Deputy Bolan shrugged. "He's been eating less and less. That's why we brought in the big guns today. I guess he's gotten depressed and lost his appetite."

Wyatt pondered this. "Granger, lose his appetite? That'd

be a first." He watched his brother carefully through the window. "Hey buddy, you need your strength, especially to sustain your wolf form for so long. You need to eat, brother."

I kneeled beside Wyatt and peered inside. The wolf's eyes were closed. "Sheriff, can you hear me?"

No response. His ears didn't even perk up like they usually did in response to my voice.

I turned back to the others. "I think he might be sick."

The deputy squished in between us. "You might be right, Ember." He pulled out his phone. "I'm going to call the healer's office and get Cephas in here."

"He's a druid," Wyatt told me. "One of the healers in town."

"Yes, I remember."

The deputy tucked away his phone. "Cephas is on the way."

"What about Alec?" I asked. "Has he shown any signs of illness?"

"Not that I've noticed. You're welcome to check on him."

I hesitated. I wasn't sure if I wanted to see Alec, not when he'd specifically asked me to stay away. I felt compelled to follow his orders. Highly unusual for me. Then again, I didn't normally take orders from someone with teeth for weapons.

"I'll leave it to you," I said. "I'd like to see what the healer can do for Sheriff Nash."

Wyatt wiggled his eyebrows. "Fond of my brother, are you? I think the feeling is mutual."

I glared at Wyatt. "I'm nothing more than a concerned citizen."

Wyatt studied me. "Yes. I see the concern written all over that pretty face. Your mother's face, I imagine. You don't have the look of a Rose."

I bristled. "Yes, yes. So I've been told."

It didn't take long for the druid to arrive. He was a stout

man with a shining bald head. He wore a brown cloak and shoes that resembled moccasins.

"Cephas, thank you for coming so quickly," the deputy said.

The druid looked at me with surprise. "The Rose girl?"

I nodded.

"Welcome home," he said, and hurried past me to the sealed door. "You'll need to let me in, Deputy Bolan. I can't heal anyone from the other side of a door. I'm good, but I'm not that good."

"Yes, of course." The deputy unlocked the door and opened it wide enough for the healer to slip through, not that there was any chance of the wolf escaping. He appeared far too weak and disinterested.

Three faces pressed together, trying to watch the druid at work. I'd never seen a healer in action, so I watched with as much fascination as genuine concern. First, he waved his hands over the wolf without touching him. Then he began muttering an incantation as he pressed his palms against the wolf's back.

"What's the diagnosis?" Wyatt asked. "Is he going to live?"

"He's been lupine too long," the druid said, running his hands through the wolf's fur. "His body is having trouble coping. His system is breaking down."

"What can we do?" I asked.

"I'm doing it now," Cephas said, concentrating on the sheriff. "This should do the trick. Now, please be quiet and let me work."

We quieted and observed the druid as he continued to chant and run his hands over the wolf's body. I didn't understand the words, although I recognized them as different from the language of the witches.

The thick coat of the wolf receded and the four-legged body contorted, producing the sheriff's human form in the fetal position on the floor. He shivered and I ran to fetch a jacket I'd seen hanging on a hook.

I returned quickly and handed the jacket to Cephas. "Is he going to be okay?"

The druid covered the sheriff's naked body. "Yes, I believe so." He glanced at the deputy. "We should move him somewhere more comfortable now."

"On it," Deputy Bolan replied.

"What about Alec?" I inquired.

Cephas bowed his head. "I don't see how I can help him. I'd need to get close enough to touch him."

There had to be a way. We couldn't heal the sheriff but leave Alec to rot. "What if the deputy tranquilizes him? Then you can go in and try to heal him."

Deputy Bolan reappeared with two trolls holding a stretcher between them. They lifted the sheriff onto the stretcher and carted him out of the cell.

"Where will you take him?" I asked.

"There's a bed upstairs," the deputy said. "He can recuperate there until he's well enough to go home."

Cephas stood and dusted off his hands. "Can you assist in making the vampire unconscious?"

The leprechaun smiled. "It would be my pleasure."

I accompanied the druid and the deputy to Alec's adjacent cell. Deputy Bolan produced the same tranquilizer gun the sheriff had used to subdue Alec in the newspaper office.

"How are you going to get an accurate shot through that narrow slit?" I asked.

The deputy gave a disappointed shake of his head. "O ye of little faith. I'm trained for this sort of thing."

"To shoot prisoners in their cells?" I asked, incredulous.

Deputy Bolan rolled his beady eyes. "I meant difficult shots." He tapped on the door and pulled over a step stool so that he could peer through the slit. "Hello, Alec."

"Deputy," came Alec's cordial voice.

"I'm going to have to shoot you," the deputy said. "Cephas thinks he can heal you, but we need you to be unconscious."

Alec's sigh was barely audible. "I understand. Do what you must."

"I'm right here," I said, careful not to knock the leprechaun off the step stool. "I'll make sure he doesn't pull any funny business."

Deputy Bolan glared at me. "What kind of funny business do you think I would pull in this situation?"

"I have no idea," I said. "This is all new to me."

"Aim for the chest," Alec said, and I heard a rustle of movement. "The effect will be quicker."

"Thank you," Deputy Bolan said. He aimed and fired off the tranquilizer.

I held my breath, waiting to hear the thud as his body hit the ground. I winced when it happened.

"He didn't hurt himself, did he?" I asked.

"He's a vampire," Deputy Bolan said. "He'll heal quickly from any physical injuries." The deputy unlocked the cell and Cephas moved inside to work his druid magic.

Deputy Bolan grabbed the door to close it, but I stopped him.

"We don't want to lock Cephas in," I said. "What if there's a problem?"

"Fine," the deputy huffed. "I'm going to check on the sheriff. Bring Alec upstairs when it's done, assuming he's conscious and healed."

I nodded, my gaze fixed on the druid. What an amazing skill to have. I had no idea what Cephas was doing, but it looked impressive. When Alec stirred, my body stiffened. What if he was still in his heightened state and grabbed Cephas? How would I be able to help him?

My fears were unnecessary. When Alec finally sat up, I

recognized the polished editor-in-chief I'd come to know. He immediately straightened his cuff links and my body relaxed.

"My utmost gratitude," he said to the healer.

"I'm glad to be of service," Cephas replied. "How do you feel?"

"Like myself," Alec said. He rose to his feet and his gaze met mine. "Miss Rose, I am deeply sorry for what I've put you through."

"You didn't put me through anything," I said. "I'm just glad you're okay. Let's go upstairs and show Deputy Bolan that you're back to normal."

We reached the top of the staircase. "You speak to the deputy. I've been gone far too long and have much to take care of." Alec flinched. "I…I'm dreadfully embarrassed by my behavior. You must have been very frightened."

"I was," I admitted. "But I knew you were lurking in there and that something was wrong."

He glanced away, unable to look me in the eye. "Yet another reason it's best to keep a safe distance. My capacity to hurt you is far too great."

"Alec," I said. I wanted to tell him he was being ridiculous, but was he? I mean, he was right—he could have killed me. One slip and I'd have been his next meal.

He shook his head. "Trust me. It is for the best, Miss Rose." He brushed past me and strode down the corridor without a backward glance.

I watched him go, fighting back tears. Why did his decision bother me so much? How could I cry over the loss of something I never had in the first place?

"You okay, Rose?"

I blinked. The sheriff stood in the corridor, fully dressed and looking back to his usual swaggering self.

"Thank goodness," I said, heaving a sigh.

He grinned. "Aw shucks. Don't tell me you were worried about me."

"Of course I was worried. This town needs a sheriff," I said. "In case you haven't noticed, there always seems to be something bad happening."

His grin vanished. "Right. Well, I'm back now. No cause for alarm."

"You should go home and rest," I said.

"Don't tell me what to do, Rose," he replied. "As you said, I'm the sheriff and I'll decide what's best."

"Typical male," I said hotly. "Fine, you decide what's best, even though you were shaking violently on the floor less than half an hour ago." I waved my hands in the air. "Never mind that I saw you turn in front of me and eye me like I was the prey you'd been stalking."

He shoved his hands in his pockets. "Yeah. Sorry about that. It isn't typical behavior for me. Part of the curse." He cocked his head. "Deputy Bolan says you two have been tracking leads."

"Unsuccessfully," I said. "We needed to go broader. We were too busy trying to tie the victims together, but I don't think that's what's happening."

"You think it's someone wanting to cause general chaos?" he queried.

"Not chaos," I said. "Maybe directing their anger at the town in general. More random. You happened to be in the wrong place at the wrong time, same as the others."

He peered at me. "What about you? You were in all these wrong places at all the wrong times. Why weren't you cursed?"

"Trust me. I've been trying to figure that out." Along with the Round Table of Old Folks.

The sheriff shifted his stance, like he was trying to decide whether to say something. "So, thanks for coming to visit me when I was…unwell. The conscious part of me knew you were there…and appreciated it."

"It was no trouble," I said. "Alec was here, too. I was able to keep tabs on both of you."

He grunted. "Right. Of course." He gave me a wave. "See you around, Rose."

"Take care of yourself, Sheriff."

CHAPTER 16

Now that the sheriff and Alec were back to their usual selves, I decided to make good on my promise to show up at the Starry Hollow tourism office. On my way up the steps, a man pushed past me and I nearly fell over. Back in the human world, I would have taken him to task for his rude behavior, but in a paranormal town, I worried that I'd piss off the wrong magic user and end up a frog.

Thaddeus, a centaur that worked in the tourism office, awaited me at the top of the steps.

"Who was that?" I asked.

Thaddeus wiped the steam from his glasses. "Noah Sturgeon. Don't mind him. He was recently let go from his job at the Starry Hollow Power Plant. He's been raging at everyone he comes in contact with."

I followed Thaddeus into the charming building.

"Is he a magic user?"

Thaddeus frowned. "Noah? He's a berserker."

"A ber-what-er?"

"A berserker. A descendants of the warriors that once served Odin."

I hated to ask my next question. "Who's Odin?"

Thaddeus rubbed his forehead. "I just have to remind myself that it's not your fault. You're from New Jersey."

I held out my hands in an innocent gesture. "That's right. I am completely blameless for my ignorance."

"Odin is a Norse god. His warriors were lunatics on the battlefield. They were well known for their wild natures."

I glanced at the door where Noah had just departed. "So Noah may have inherited an insanity gene?"

"Apparently, he was fired for insubordination. His manager had had enough of Noah's outbursts on the job."

"Can he do magic?" I asked.

"If he can, I've never seen any evidence of it," Thaddeus said.

Hmm. If someone was cursing residents out of anger or frustration, it was unlikely he'd hire someone to perform the magic. That would be too calculated, too premeditated. As much as I hated to end up with another dead end, I ruled out Noah.

"So, what's on the agenda today?" I asked, ready to get to work.

"I'm glad you're here," he said. "We received the final entries for the artwork to match the new town slogan."

"Do you have a favorite?" I asked.

"I do." He beckoned me to his desk, where three papers had been placed side by side. Each one incorporated the slogan—*Come to Starry Hollow, where spells were made to be broken.* The first image was of a wand broken in half and surrounded by glitter. The middle one was a picture of the Painted Pixies, the famous row of colorful houses. The third one was an image of the ocean in front of the old pub, the Whitethorn.

"This is so cool," I said. "I can't believe you're actually going ahead with my slogan idea."

"It took a fair amount of cajoling to convince Aster," he admitted, "but thankfully she's not as stubborn as her mother."

I bit back a smile. My aunt had referred to both my father and me as stubborn and had made it clear it wasn't a compliment.

"It's worth a try," I said. "If it doesn't catch on, there's no real harm."

"If nothing else, it gave Florian something to do."

My eyebrows shot up. "Florian drew these?"

Thaddeus nodded. "He's been very busy on our behalf. I think that's the main reason Aster decided to go ahead with your slogan idea. She could see that Florian was enthusiastic about it."

Good for Florian. Of course, I knew his real motivation was the boat he was promised, but still. He was making a genuine effort and that was all his mother really wanted.

"What else has he been doing?" I pictured him turning up to flirt with any unsuspecting tourists who happened by.

"He went through our entire inventory and made suggestions on what he thought was missing, based on his own travel experience."

"Anything worthwhile?"

Thaddeus tilted his head. "As a matter of fact, there were several gems and Aster approved them." He chuckled. "Naturally, one of his ideas involved women's clothing. More skimpy tops with the new slogan across the chest."

I rolled my eyes. "His mother will have a fit. She'll shred a kaftan at the thought of Starry Hollow being seen as low brow."

"His mother isn't privy to the details here," Thaddeus said. "Which is probably for the best."

The door flew open and Aster came in, looking every inch the Targaryen supermodel witch that she was. "Sorry

I'm late. I had to make an unexpected pit stop to console a friend."

"It's no hair off my tail," Thaddeus said. "Ember and I were just discussing the artwork Florian provided for the slogan."

Aster smiled at me. "Can you believe it? I'm so pleased he's taking a genuine interest in something."

It was nice to see her happy about her brother's involvement for a change. Usually, she was grumbling about him under her breath.

"I'm amazed he can draw so well," I said. "I didn't realize he had any hidden talents."

"That's partly what's so frustrating about him," Aster said. "Florian is good at so many things. He could close his eyes, pluck an activity out of the air, and master it with little effort. It causes him to lose interest quickly."

"He likes a challenge," I said. That explained the heavy rotation of women. "You know, I hadn't thought of it before, but he and Marley are alike in many ways. She doesn't have her magic yet, but she's good at everything. I can see over time how that might take its toll."

Aster adjusted her pearl earring. "We should have them spend more time together. Maybe they can challenge each other."

"Marley is very fond of Florian," I said. She was horrified when he was trapped in frog form. At the memory of the frog spell, my thoughts turned to Alec. "You know what else we should have in here? A section with Alec Hale's books. We should celebrate the fact that a famous author lives and works here."

Aster scrunched her perfect nose. "Do you think Alec would like that, though? I've always been under the impression that he prefers his anonymity."

"I'll ask him now that he's on the mend," I said.

Aster smiled. "You look so relieved that he's recovered. I think Mother is concerned about your obvious affection for one another."

Thaddeus glanced at me in surprise. "Affection? Alec Hale? Surely not."

"He's a very nice vampire," I said. "Let's not make more out of this than it is."

"Of course, Mother is *far* more concerned about Sheriff Nash," Aster said. "She has very little tolerance for were-wolves and the Nash brothers in particular. She would have been perfectly content to see him remain a werewolf and have the council appoint a new sheriff."

"I, for one, am glad he's back in human form," I said. I'd seen a side of both men recently that unnerved me. Even though I *knew* that the sheriff was a werewolf and Alec was a vampire, they'd seemed entirely human until the curse revealed otherwise.

Aster's phone buzzed and she fished it out of her handbag to glance at the screen. "Oh no. It's Everly again."

"Who's Everly?" I asked.

"The fairy friend I had to console on the way in," Aster said. "I told her to call me anytime. She must be seriously out of sorts to think I meant it."

"I have a bad habit of taking things at face value, too," I said. "Why is she out of sorts?"

"Her fiancé called off their wedding two weeks ago," Aster said. "She's been spiraling down toward rock bottom ever since."

A fairy off her rocker? That sounded promising. "You know, Aster. I'd be happy to talk to her if you're too busy."

Aster studied me. "Why would you do that? It's draining to talk about other people's problems."

"When Karl died, I didn't have any close friends to talk to about it," I said. "You tend to lose your peer group when you get pregnant and married light-years ahead of everyone else." I was always too busy struggling to make a living to care. When your priority was feeding your child, there was little energy left over for self-pity.

"So you think helping Everly will somehow help you?" Aster queried.

Sure, let's go with that. "Let me take something off your plate," I said, appealing to her ego. "You already do so much for the community."

"Okay then. She lives over in the White Oak neighborhood," Aster said. "The pink house with the turquoise door."

"She's not at work at this hour?"

Aster shook her white-blond head. "She took a leave of absence. She's been struggling to function. Very depressed. Cephas tried to offer her some herbal remedies to take the edge off her dark mood, but she refused."

A fairy with a lot of time on her hands and a depressed attitude. Very promising, indeed.

"I'll report back later," I said.

"Good luck," Thaddeus called.

"Thanks," I yelled. If I couldn't get to the bottom of this nightmare curse soon, we were going to need all the luck we could get.

I stood in front of the pink house with the turquoise door, marveling at the sight. If ever there was a house designed for a fairy, this was it. There was an actual rainbow arched over the house and the flowers and bushes were covered in glitter.

I knocked on the door, still mesmerized by my surroundings. It was like driving through New Jersey neighborhoods at Christmastime when everyone's houses were decorated with lights and garish plastic Santas.

The door opened and Everly fluttered before me, a hot pink eye mask pulled up like a headband.

She squinted when she saw me. "Who are you?" She sucked in a dramatic breath. "Oh sweet sugar plums, you're not his new girlfriend, are you?"

"I'm Aster's cousin, Ember," I said. "She asked me to check on you."

Everly relaxed. "I guess she had something more important to do. She *always* has something important to do."

A chip on her shoulder. Everly was looking better and better.

"Can I come in?" I asked.

"Sure. What do I care? My life is over anyway." She fluttered into the house and I followed.

The interior was in stark contrast to the outside. The blinds were drawn and there were dirty cups and plates scattered throughout the room. She and Montague were a match made in messy heaven.

"You don't know Scott, do you?" she asked, sprawling across the sofa. She plumped the pillow under her head. "If you ever meet him, run in the opposite direction. He's a filthy piece of minotaur shit."

I sat in the recliner opposite her. "Aster said he broke off your engagement two weeks ago. What happened?"

Everly pulled down her eye mask. "It was so unexpected. Everything was fine. We were both excited about the wedding. We'd booked the honeymoon."

"And he just called off the wedding out of the blue?" I queried.

"He didn't call it off explicitly," she said. "He just didn't show up for the final fitting for his tux. I called and texted, but he didn't respond. He didn't answer the door at home. I thought he was hurt. I even called the healer's office." Tears streamed out from under the eye mask, staining her cheeks.

"So what happened?"

"He finally replied to my frantic text where I threatened bodily harm if he didn't respond."

Ah. A fairy after my own heart. "Did he explain what was going on?"

"Not really. He only said he was sorry and that it wasn't going to work."

My heart went out to her. What a crappy way to be dumped. "He didn't even have the gonads to tell you to your face?"

She wiped her cheeks free of tears. "No. I couldn't even get him to elaborate. As far as I knew, we were really happy. I didn't even realize he was having second thoughts."

"I'm sorry, Everly. That's rough."

"I had to cancel the wedding plans by myself. Try and explain to my friends." She gulped for air. "How could I explain something that I didn't understand myself?"

"Have you seen him since the text?" I asked.

"No, he refuses to see me." She started to cry again. "I think it's too hard for him. He doesn't deal with emotions very well."

"Yours or his own?"

"Both. It took forever for me to break down his wall." She paused. "I guess I didn't do as good of a job as I thought."

"You couldn't know what was happening in his head if he didn't share it with you, Everly," I said. "You're not a mind reader." That was one advantage some witches had over fairies. They had glitter. We had psychic skills. I knew which one I preferred.

"I planned my whole future with him," she sobbed. "What am I supposed to do now?"

I sighed. This was one subject I had experience with. "Yard by yard, life is hard. Inch by inch, life is a cinch."

She flipped up her eye mask and looked at me. "What kind of human mumbo jumbo is that?"

I shrugged. "It got me through a lot of dark days."

Everly took a renewed interest in me. "What kind of dark days?"

"My husband died a few years ago and I became a single mother in the blink of an eye. No warning. No time to prepare. One day he kissed me goodbye and never came home." I snapped my fingers. "Life as we knew it was over. My daughter wants me to date, but I haven't been able to move on."

Everly gaped at me. "Glitter and gold, that's terrible."

I ignored the ache in my heart. "Life can be terrible sometimes. We have no control. But you know what? Life can also be amazing."

"How can you say that?" she asked, visibly shaken. "Your husband *died*. You had your whole lives ahead of you to share."

"That's the terrible part," I agreed. "But then, one day out of the blue, three ridiculously gorgeous people showed up in my apartment with crazy magical powers and saved my life." I snapped my fingers again. "Just like that, everything changed for the better. That's the amazing part."

She pulled her knees up to her chest. "I have a rainbow over my house. That's pretty amazing."

"It really is. How'd you do it?"

"Fairy magic," she said. "I taught myself. It's a difficult spell. A lot of my friends are totally jealous."

So she was a fairly talented fairy. It was time for my big question, though I hated to ask. She seemed so vulnerable right now.

"You haven't been doing any magic while you're under emotional strain, have you?"

"Gods, no," she replied. "I can barely get out of bed in the morning. I haven't showered in..." She bit her lip. "Never mind."

"You're a beautiful fairy, Everly. You'll meet someone else," I said. "Someone who values you and your relationship."

"You can't promise that," Everly replied. "Look at you. You're pretty for a witch, although a little substandard for a Rose, and you've been single for years."

"By choice," I said. "I could have had opportunities if I'd wanted them." I thought of Alec in the back of the limo and the sheriff in his office.

"Scott and I were perfect for each other," she insisted. "I don't understand how he could do this to me."

"I hate to say this, Everly, but sometimes we don't get to understand why things happen. We just need to accept that they do." Crap on a stick, that sounded profound coming out of my mouth. I must've read it somewhere.

Everly muffled a cry. "I only wanted an explanation. He owes me that much after all we've shared together. We were supposed to be getting married. How can you not be honest with the fairy you supposedly love?"

"You seem like an emotionally healthy fairy," I said. *Present circumstances aside.* "It seems to me that maybe Scott doesn't have your communication skills. He copes with issues in a different way."

"In a *stupid* way," Everly grumbled.

"No argument there," I said. "Everly, you may have dodged a bullet with Scott. Unless he was willing to do some real work on himself, your marriage was doomed before it even began."

Slowly, she slid her eye mask over her head. "You really think so?"

I nodded emphatically. "You need to find someone who doesn't run for cover at the slightest whiff of a problem.

Someone strong enough to come to you and talk through problems. Scott isn't that person."

Everly sat up and sniffed. "Thanks, Ember. I hadn't thought about it that way, but you're right. It would have made it impossible to work through any issues. And what if we'd had kids by the time I wanted out?" She heaved a sigh. "What a blessing in disguise."

My work here was done. Everly clearly wasn't the culprit and I'd helped her through a rough patch. Go me.

"If you don't mind," she said, "I think I'd like to take a shower."

I gave her an encouraging smile. "I'll show myself out."

As I left the White Oak neighborhood, I ran into—of all people—Milo Jarvis.

"Miss Rose," he greeted me, clearly embarrassed to see me again. It was understandable, considering I'd seen him naked. Come to think of it, I'd seen a lot of naked residents this month. Good thing I wasn't a prude.

"Hi, Milo. How's Big Dreams?"

"Terrific now that we have the funding from your family's foundation." His brow creased. "We did have a sad bit of news, though. One of our families lost their teenaged son. I've just come from paying my respects." He shook his head. "Bless them. They're really struggling."

"What happened?"

"He'd been critically injured six months ago in a broomstick accident and we'd hoped he would pull through." Milo sighed deeply. "In the end, his injures were too severe."

My stomach knotted. "A broomstick accident?" No way was I telling Marley about that guy. She'd never get on a broomstick again.

"He wasn't a wizard, if that's what you're wondering. He

was an elf who'd been messing around with magic. He lacked the proper training for magic or broomsticks."

"Why did he want to ride a broomstick?" I asked.

"Apparently, it was the result of a dare. He'd been with friends, drinking too much ale in the woods. One of them thought it would be funny to swipe a broomstick from a witch's house."

My heart sank at the stupidity of youth. And this poor elf and his family were now paying the ultimate price.

"What was his name?" I asked.

"Stephen Caldwell," Milo replied. "We'd granted their wish to have a dog. Stephen had always wanted one, but his parents refused because they didn't trust him to look after it."

A dog. Young Stephen was my kind of people.

"Would it be weird if I stopped by to see them?" I asked.

Milo patted his brow with a handkerchief. "Honestly, I think they'd be grateful for any diversion right now. They seem to be sniping at each other. I sensed a lot of unresolved anger. I suggested counseling, but I can't force them to attend."

I sensed a lot of unresolved anger echoed in my head. It was worth a shot.

"I'll see what I can do," I said.

"They live two blocks over on Alchemy Avenue. Brick house with a green door."

I had just enough time to squeeze in a visit to the Caldwells, especially if there was a chance it would yield the information we'd been looking for.

I located the house easily enough and prepared myself for the misery within its walls. Stephen's father invited me in and I recognized the haze of depression as soon as I stepped across the threshold. It had a different quality from Everly's dramatic repose. Grief saturated the room and my heart

167

seized when I saw the two younger elves seated on the sofa, staring at their tablet screens like zombies.

"I'm Stephen's father, Jayson," the older elf said. "This is my wife, Lolly, and our sons, Rudy and Clark."

A mid-sized yellow dog bounded into the room and began jumping in front of me, eager to make my acquaintance. He had Labrador qualities but seemed to be a blend of breeds.

"And that's Sweeney," Jayson said. "A gift from Big Dreams."

"Nice to meet you all," I said, bending to pet the dog's head. "My name is Ember and Big Dreams is the reason I'm here. My family contributes to Big Dreams. I ran into Milo Jarvis a few minutes ago and he told me your sad story. I'd like to offer my condolences."

"That's kind of you," Lolly said. "We haven't had the outpouring of support some folks get, probably because Stephen brought this upon himself."

"That's a bit harsh, Lolly," Jayson said. "He was a kid, making immature decisions."

"Exactly," Lolly said. "He didn't die of an illness or at the hands of someone else. It was his own doing."

Jayson shushed her, glancing over his shoulder at the two younger elves. "We have discussed this. It isn't healthy for the boys."

"It wasn't healthy for the boys to show them magic either," she shot back, "but that didn't stop you from doing it anyway."

"You taught him magic?" I queried.

Lolly folded her arms. "Milo didn't tell you that part, did he? Stephen was interested in magic because of his father. Jayson brought home a grimoire from the secondhand bookstore and decided it would be a good idea to try and teach the boys."

I knew from other paranormals that elves *could* learn magic, even though they weren't born magic users. Some were able to tap into Nature's magical energy and make it work for them, despite not being born with the ability.

"What about his friends?" I asked. "Were they magic users?"

"They were a mixed bag," Lolly said. "A troll, another elf, and a goblin."

"They all thought it would be fun to do spells," Jayson said.

"Of course they did. Everything sounds fun when you're wasted in the woods with your friends," Lolly said.

Wow. The room was brimming with anger and resentment. No wonder the two boys were comatose on the sofa. They were probably adept at blocking out the arguments by now.

"Do you know any magic?" I asked Lolly. She was clearly the angrier of the two.

"Absolutely not," she replied. "I'm an elf and I'm perfectly content with that. I'm not the one always looking for greener grass."

Jayson's jaw clenched. "Lolly, this isn't the time."

I rubbed behind Sweeney's ear. "You know, I think the dog needs to go out. If someone grabs his leash, I'm happy to take him outside."

"I'll get it," Jayson said, retrieving a leash from a nearby hook. "And I'll go with you. Sometimes staying inside can be suffocating." He shot a menacing glance at his wife.

I hooked the dog and followed Jayson outside, closing the door behind us. We walked around the lawn, letting Sweeney sniff the flowers along the border.

"Sorry about that," he said. "We've been very upset, as you can imagine."

"It's understandable," I said. "You've suffered a horrible

loss. It must be a nightmare for you." A real nightmare they can never wake up from, as opposed to the fleeting nightmares of the curse.

"I never thought dabbling in magic would lead to this," Jayson said. "It was meant to be harmless fun. A diversion from our mundane lives."

It was strange to listen to a Starry Hollow elf describe his life as mundane.

"My wife blames me," he said.

We stopped walking so the dog could pee.

"How about you?" I asked.

"I don't blame myself," Jayson said, after a moment of consideration.

"Do you blame anyone? I would understand if you did. After my husband died, I walked around with a lot of misdirected anger. Road rage was my middle name. One time, I even yelled at a bank teller for running out of lollipops."

"I've had a little bit of that," Jayson admitted. "I yelled at a car for driving too fast down our street. I was walking Sweeney and the high speed spooked the dog. I'll be honest, though, we got Sweeney for Stephen, but he's been a comfort to all of us."

The dog looked up at us, as though he knew he was the topic of conversation.

"Sweeney slept with Stephen every night until he died," Jayson said. "Now he sleeps with the boys."

"That's nice," I said. "He's become a member of the family. My dog is the same. I can't imagine life without him."

"Whenever I feel the anger bubbling up, I hug the dog," Jayson said. "Don't I, boy?"

I studied Jayson as he stooped to rub the dog's back. Despite their upsetting circumstances, I highly doubted Jayson was to blame for the nightmare curse. He wasn't unhinged enough, or magically talented enough, to be the source of the curse. It was obvious the family needed help, though.

"I'm glad the dog is helping you all, but I'm going to risk overstepping my boundary and recommend counseling for your family."

Jayson tugged on his pointy ear. "You wouldn't be the first person to suggest it."

"Your family is struggling, Jayson. Believe me, I get it, but don't try to deal with it alone. You have two other sons who deserve a well-adjusted childhood."

"Did you go to counseling?" Jayson asked. "After your husband died?"

"If I could have afforded it, I would have," I said. "My insurance didn't cover it."

"We don't have to worry about insurance here," he said.

"I know. That's one of the perks of a Starry Hollow passport. You're very fortunate." And now so was I.

"I don't know if Lolly will go," he said, with an awkward glance back at the house.

"Then start without her," I said. "Go by yourself and then add members of the family as it feels appropriate."

He regarded me carefully. "Are you a therapist, by any chance?"

I laughed. Loudly. "Trust me, Jayson. You do *not* want me trying to guide anyone through an emotional crisis. I'm the worst."

The elf took the leash from me and patted my hand. "You should give yourself more credit than that, Ember. It seems to me you're doing just fine."

CHAPTER 17

WITH THE PERPETRATOR of the nightmare curse still at large, it was difficult to focus on a task as tedious as perfecting my scribbles. It was like learning to sew in the middle of a forest fire.

"You've not been practicing your runes," Hazel scolded me. She scrutinized the paper on the table. "This looks like you handed the dog a pen and told him to go to town."

"That's insulting," I said, snatching the paper away. "PP3 suffers from arthritis. And I worked very hard on this."

"If by 'very hard,' you mean drunk at three in the morning with your daughter's ink stamp, then I agree with you."

"Mistress-of-Runecraft, my eye," I said. "You wouldn't recognize true genius if it jumped up and bit you on your red nose."

"Red nose?"

My hand flew to cover my mouth. Although I referred to Hazel as a crazed clown in my head, I'd never actually let my thoughts slip out before.

"Red. You know, like your hair."

She narrowed her eyes. "Last I checked, my nose is not

the same color as my hair. Forget three in the morning. I think you might be drunk now."

I waved her off. "Get on with the lesson, Hazel. I've got incantations to practice, too. Aunt Hyacinth insists that magic training comes first. The coven is becoming a real drain on my system."

"That's because you're expending too much energy playing the sheriff's sidekick. He's already got one of those, you know. His name is Deputy Bolan."

"I'm not playing his sidekick," I insisted. "I'm trying to get to the bottom of a bad situation. One that has me looking like the town fear monger."

Hazel placed a judgmental hand on her hip. "That would certainly explain Marley's anxiety."

"Marley's anxiety has nothing to do with me," I said. "Not to mention she's improved a lot since we came here. Sleeps in her own bed and everything." Sometimes.

"Still. I'm sure the fact that you're easily scared doesn't help matters."

I fixed her with my hard stare. "I said fear *monger*. That means I'm the one who spreads the fear. Maybe if I wrote it in runes you'd understand." I lifted my pen to draw a mock example.

"Whom are you trying to convince?" she asked. "Me or you?"

"I am *not* easily scared," I said through gritted teeth.

Fists pounded on the door, causing both of us to jump. My pen flew out of my hand and landed on PP3's back. He yelped and growled at the naughty pen, now on the floor.

"Ember, come quickly." I heard Florian's muffled voice through the door.

I jerked open the door. "What's wrong?"

Florian's cheeks were flushed. "It's the story of a lifetime.

You've got to cover it for the paper." He was almost breathless.

"What's the story of a lifetime?" I queried.

"There's a...Forget it. You've got to see it to believe it." He held out his hand. "Come on. I've got Book and Candle saddled. It'll be easier to go through the woods."

Now my curiosity was piqued. "Hazel? Class is over, right?"

Hazel begrudgingly packed away the Big Book of Scribbles. "One of these days you will focus on runecraft, Ember Rose. Your aunt specifically wants you to master this skill."

"My aunt wants me to master all the skills, so she can brag about me at Back to School Night, or whatever the coven equivalent is. It's not about me. It's about the Rose legacy."

Florian shrugged at Hazel. "What can I say? She's very astute. Now let's go."

Hazel threw up her hands in defeat. "See you next week. Next time have your homework done properly."

I hurried out the door and stood beside the massive white horse. "Remember, Candle. I need your help. Still not an equestrian expert."

Candle lowered her body to the ground, making it easier for me to climb on.

Florian watched in disbelief. "How did you get the horse to do that?"

"The art of conversation," I said.

"You know that's not normal, right?" he asked.

"Neither is using magic to dump me in the saddle, so I guess we're both guilty of unusual methods."

"Good point." He mounted the horse with the grace of a dancer. Show-off. "Onward, Book!"

The horses raced across the grounds of the estate and through the woods. Long, thin strands of my hair blew into my eyes and mouth. This was not as sexy as it looked on television. I should have grabbed a brush on my way out.

We passed the pond where Florian had recently spent time as a frog and I noticed him give the place a longing look as we continued forward. Apparently, you could take the boy out of the frog, but you couldn't take the frog out of the boy.

"Where are we going?" I asked.

"The far end of town," he replied. "It's chaos over there."

Through the thickness of the trees, I spotted a footbridge over one of several local streams that led to the ocean. A flash of color caught my attention.

"Florian, someone's running onto the bridge," I said. I steered Candle closer for a better look. I recognized the figure. He stopped running when he saw us.

"Don't come any closer," he yelled.

"Cephas?" I nudged the horse and she lowered me to the ground.

"It must be coming this way," Florian said.

"What's coming this way?" Whatever it was, it couldn't be good. The druid healer looked absolutely terrified.

"I'm going to see if I can stop it," Florian said. Without waiting for me to respond, he galloped further into the woods.

"Stay here," I told Candle and turned back to Cephas.

"You need to go back," the druid yelled. "Don't come this way." He glanced over his shoulder, petrified.

I walked slowly toward him on the bridge. The wooden planks beneath my feet began to tremble and I looked around quizzically. What was happening? I looked at the stream below and noticed a slight ripple in the water. Something felt wrong. The hair on the back of my neck stood on end.

"By the gods," Cephas whispered. "It's following me." His

face paled and I was afraid he was about to throw himself off the bridge into the water.

"Cephas, what's wrong?"

He was frozen in place. I looked past him just as a giant oblong object trailed through the sky toward us. It landed on the bridge with a splatter, shaking the entire structure. We jumped back, clutching each other.

"Is that what I think it is?" Scattered on the bridge were fragments of a decorated shell. Pastel pink, yellow, and green.

"Duck," Cephas yelled, yanking me down with him.

"Are you sure?" I queried. "The egg looks way too big..."

Another colorful egg flew over our heads and exploded on the ground beyond the bridge.

"Easter egg grenades?" I queried.

The bridge shook again. Popcorn balls. We were under attack with nowhere to hide.

"Cephas, have you been cursed?" I asked. That would explain why *it* was following him into the woods.

The druid nodded. "I tried to lead it away from busy areas, so I ran into the woods. Now I don't know what to do."

That made two of us. "What's your worst nightmare, Cephas? Broken eggs?"

We huddled on the bridge together and Cephas spoke to me in a state of panic. "When I was a child, I begged my parents to adopt some of the human customs. One of them was Easter. I wanted to dye eggs and have the Easter Bunny hide them for me to find the next day."

That sounded innocent enough. What was so frightening about it? "So what happened?"

"My parents decided to go the extra mile. They had a friend dress in an Easter bunny costume and sneak into the house to hide the eggs while I was asleep. What they didn't know was that I had awoken in the night to find a huge six-foot bunny at the foot of my bed. I screamed, scaring the bunny, and the basket of eggs flew everywhere. One hit me in the head and cracked. I was so traumatized afterward, I had nightmares for years about being attacked by the Easter Bunny."

Oh boy.

The bridge shook harder this time and I realized what was coming. Another egg sailed over our heads and landed at the foot of the bridge. Pieces of shell flew in all directions. Polka dots and stripes flashed before my eyes.

"Incoming," Cephas yelled. Another egg plummeted to the ground. This one narrowly missed us.

"Let me think of a spell," I said, squeezing my eyes closed. I tried to force myself to concentrate. The eggs were too big to control with telekinesis. I wasn't advanced enough to handle giant Easter eggs. Hell, I couldn't even move scissors back at the art gallery. I racked my brain for what other skills I had. I thought of the protective bubble that Wren had created when the branch threatened to pummel us.

I clasped the druid's hands and said, "*Vesica.*"

I felt the energy of the invisible wall as it stretched around us. The barrier formed just in time as another Easter egg careened toward us. It slammed into the protective bubble and bounced off, splashing into the water below. Its pastel stripes were visible from the bridge as the egg floated downstream.

"He's coming," Cephas said, and swallowed a sob.

I turned my head to see the giant bunny emerge from the shadows. He was not the six-foot bunny of the druid's nightmares. This bunny was the size of a five-story building. He was brown and fluffy, wearing a pale blue bow tie and carrying a wicker basket full of eggs. His buckteeth were more menacing than adorable. Ice traveled up my spine as I realized that this bunny could easily crush the bubble and us.

It was one thing to deflect eggs, but quite another to with-stand the pressure of a giant foot. Lucky rabbit's foot, my ass.

I had to think of another spell. The protective bubble wouldn't be enough.

"I can change the color of the eggs," I blurted.

Cephas inclined his head. "What good will that do?"

"I have no idea," I said, my voice shaking. "My magical skills are limited." Where was Florian? He needed to get back here and deal with this giant fluffy menace.

"I feel sick," Cephas said, and promptly vomited through a gap in the planks. Lovely.

As the Easter bunny advanced, the bridge began to sway. I quickly ran through every bit of magic I'd encountered since the night I met my cousins.

"I know what to do," I said. I reversed the bubble spell and stretched my wand toward the bunny.

"No, we need the barrier," Cephas said in a panic.

He grabbed my wand as I said, "*Glaciare.*"

"Cephas, no!"

The druid turned blue and iced over, the same as the branch had done. I pictured the branch breaking apart and falling to the ground.

"Please don't crack," I told Cephas.

He said nothing, frozen in position. I squeezed my wand and turned to face the giant bunny, ready for battle.

The bunny was gone.

"What the…?" I whipped around in a circle. There was no sign of the monstrous Easter bunny.

Florian emerged from the woods and rode toward us. "I tracked it here. Where did it go?"

I breathed a sigh of relief. "It's gone. I don't know what happened. I was going to use magic to freeze it, but I acci-dentally froze Cephas instead. The next thing I knew, the bunny was gone."

"Can you unfreeze him?" I asked. I was too nervous to try. Accidentally freezing him was bad enough. What if I managed to hurt the town healer?

Florian touched Cephas lightly on his frozen shoulder and said, "*Tabescere.*"

The druid returned to his natural color, albeit a bit paler. He slumped to the ground. "Is it gone?"

"It is," I said. "It's okay, Cephas."

"I'm very thirsty," he said. "Does anyone have water?"

The mention of his thirst triggered a memory. I ran back through all the victims. I was fairly certain they'd all expressed the need for a drink at some point during the curse.

Florian snapped his fingers and produced a bottle of water for the druid. Cephas gulped it down greedily.

"Sick baby Elvis," I said. "It isn't me. I'm not the cause."

Cephas sat on the ground beside me, breathing heavily. "I never believed you were, Ember."

"I didn't want to believe it," I said, "but the evidence was becoming too much to ignore."

Florian lifted the druid off the ground and placed him in the saddle. "I'll take Cephas to his office. Help thaw him out the rest of the way."

"Yes, my assistant will be there," the druid said. "She can help."

"Perfect," Florian said with a wink. "I'd love an excuse to see Lyssa McTavish again."

"She's not interested in you," I said. "She thinks you're lazy."

"You don't bother with sugarcoating, do you?" Florian asked in his usual good-natured way. His laidback attitude was one thing I really liked about him.

"Life's too short." As I said the words, I realized how late it was. "Florian, can you ask Simon to collect Marley from school? I won't have enough time to make my stops and get back to Bailiwick Road for the final bell."

"Why? Where are you going?" my cousin asked.

"To see Milo Jarvis," I said. "I think he has the information we need to end this once and for all."

CHAPTER 18

It didn't take me long to track down the person I wanted to see on Potions Lane. As I was about to enter the apartment building, a familiar voice called my name.

I whipped around. "Sheriff?"

"You should have called me, Rose," he said. "You're dealing with things you don't understand."

"How did you know I was here?"

"Florian texted me that you were going to see Milo. I just missed you there."

I should have been annoyed, but, secretly, I was relieved to see the sheriff walking around in his human form again. That shiny star on his shirt never looked so good.

"I don't know if my theory is right," I said. "I wanted to confirm before I spoke to you."

He gave me a lopsided grin. "Are you admitting you might be wrong?"

"What I'm admitting is that this is only a theory."

"Well, I'll admit it's a decent one."

We located number sixteen and I took a deep breath before knocking. I desperately wanted to be right about this.

To end these nightmares before something far worse than a Godzilla-sized Easter bunny terrorized the town.

The door opened to reveal an older elf with large, round glasses and a pallid complexion.

"Mr. Gunnar?" I said.

He squinted. "Yes? Do I know you?"

Sheriff Nash muscled his way in front of me. "You know me, Bjorn. Could we have a word?"

"Of course, Sheriff." Bjorn pulled open the door to let us pass. "What can I do for you?"

We walked straight into a living area. The simple layout reminded me of my apartment in Maple Shade, New Jersey and I felt a brief pang of nostalgia.

Two children sat on the sofa, their noses buried in comic books. They glanced up at us with interest.

"Are you a real sheriff?" the smaller boy asked.

"I am," Sheriff Nash replied, tapping the star on his chest. "And what's your name?"

"These are my sons," Bjorn said. "Sven and Soren." Bjorn settled on a nearby recliner, appearing worn out from his brief round-trip journey to the door.

"I heard you went on the vacation of a lifetime recently," I said to the boys.

Their eyes lit up.

"Mistfall," Sven said, hopping up and down on the sofa. "It was amazing."

"It's a mountain town surrounded by mist," Soren added. "It's the coolest place ever. I want to live there when I grow up."

"I brought back this souvenir," Sven said, lifting a wooden toy from the coffee table. It looked like a marionette with wings. "I used my own money."

"Looks awesome," I agreed. "An excellent choice."

The sheriff sat adjacent to Bjorn. "Is Margot at work?"

Bjorn nodded. "A double shift today. She'll be dead on her feet when she gets home."

I sympathized. A sick husband and two young boys to care for. Margot Gunnar didn't have an enviable life. The trip to Mistfall was one that would have to sustain them for a very long time.

"Mr. Gunnar, when you returned from Mistfall, did you happen to have any bad dreams that you remember?" I asked. "Or maybe something happened that seemed very real but wasn't?"

Bjorn gave me a look of surprise. "I did, as a matter of fact." He removed his glasses to rub his eyes. "My teeth... They'd fallen out."

"They did," Sven said excitedly. "We saw it."

"But then later that day the teeth were back again." Bjorn wore a bemused expression. "It was the strangest experience. I assumed it was the anxiety over my illness returning after our relaxing trip."

"Did the teeth reappear after Milo Jarvis paid you a visit?" I asked.

"Yes, I believe so," Bjorn replied. Each word seemed to drain him of energy. "Milo had come by to find out how we got on in Mistfall. Such a kind man. Why do you ask?"

Sheriff Nash and I exchanged glances.

"That toy wasn't the only thing you brought back from Mistfall, I'm afraid," Sheriff Nash said. "You also came back with a parasite."

"A magical parasite," I added.

Sheriff Nash elbowed me. "That's like calling it Chinese food in China."

I glared at him. "Whatever."

The sheriff returned his focus to Bjorn. "It's called *parasitus tantibus*."

I shot him a quizzical look. "You know the name?"

The sheriff wiggled his phone. "My smart phone's pretty smart."

"When Milo left your house that day, Mr. Gunnar, the parasite went with him," I explained.

"It's made its way through town," the sheriff said. "We'd like to make sure that no one else experienced any similar living nightmares."

Bjorn glanced at the boys, who shook their heads. "Nor my wife," he said. "When we told her about my teeth, she said we'd imagined the whole thing."

"Where's the parasite now?" Sven asked, with the eagerness I'd expect of a boy his age.

"Dead," I replied. "I don't think it can survive freezing temperatures." When I accidentally froze Cephas, I killed the both parasites inside him. That was why the Easter bunny disappeared at the same time.

"It thrives in climates like Mistfall's," the sheriff added. "It isn't native to Starry Hollow. We need to be sure there aren't any more parasites wandering around from your vacation."

"No," Bjorn said, adjusting his glasses. "I was the only one with an issue. I hope I haven't caused any trouble. It was such a lovely trip."

I felt the sheriff place a hand on my arm in an attempt to silence me. He wanted Bjorn to keep his happy memories, and so did I.

"Not at all," I said. "Thank you for your help, Mr. Gunnar."

Sheriff Nash gently squeezed my arm in gratitude. That small, intimate gesture was well worth keeping my mouth shut—for once.

Since I'd been walking around town on foot all day, the

sheriff was kind enough to drive me home from the Gunnars' apartment.

"So what else did you learn about *parasitus tantibus* on your smartphone?" I asked.

"Quite a lot, actually. It explains why you were present each time but never infected."

I lifted an eyebrow. "It does?"

"Witches and wizards are immune," he said. "Something in your DNA. Fairies, too."

I let the information sink in. "But I was a carrier, wasn't I?" Not just a carrier. *The* carrier. The parasite had hitched a ride from Mistfall on Bjorn Gunnar, who passed it to Milo. From the board meeting on, though, I was the responsible party. I passed it to Bentley, Trupti, Alec, and the sheriff.

He gave me a sympathetic look. "It wasn't your fault, Rose."

"That's why I seemed to be the common factor," I said. "I basically gave the parasite a free ride around town."

He smirked. "What can I say? It had good taste."

"Very funny. If it was only one parasite, then why were you and Alec infected at the same time?"

"The cells can divide when they develop enough strength," the sheriff said.

My brain was in overdrive. "So when Cephas thought he'd healed you both, he'd done nothing except leave with both parasites." At least that one wasn't attributable to me. Small favors.

"That's why no one was infected while Alec and I were locked up," the sheriff said.

Poor Cephas. No wonder the druid's nightmare was so much larger in scope. If I hadn't frozen Cephas, the parasites would have only gotten stronger and divided again. I shuddered at the thought of the damage they could have done. We were lucky to have gotten off as easily as we did.

"At least there isn't an evil magic user on the loose," I said. "Makes your job easier." I moved to open the cottage door.

"So, Rose, I've been thinking..." The sheriff paused and stroked his chin.

"Not thinking! Did it cause you any pain? You might experience soreness after exercising a rarely used muscle."

He narrowed his eyes. "Come on, I'm about to say something nice. Don't ruin it."

I hesitated. "Do I want you to say something nice?"

His brow furrowed. "Why wouldn't you? Who doesn't want to be told nice things?"

I shrugged. "I don't know. Maybe someone who feels like she doesn't deserve it."

He shoved his hands in his pockets. His jeans were so tight, I was surprised he could fit them.

"Rose, would you like to have dinner with me one night?"

"She would," Marley called from behind the closed door.

Crap on a stick. I'd forgotten Marley was home. Then I heard PP3's low growl. Apparently, he was not on board with the werewolf.

"Be quiet and stop eavesdropping," I yelled back.

The sheriff chuckled. "Your little family is as nosy as mine."

"I don't think the pack qualifies as a little family," I said.

"True," he said. "So, are you gonna answer my question, or keep dodging it with stray observations?"

I chewed my lip. I *did* want to go out with him. I mean, who wouldn't be drawn to the body behind those tight jeans? But the thought of dating someone—of letting someone into my life. Ugh. What if it didn't work out? Marley and I had suffered so much loss already. And then there was Alec...

He seemed to sense my ambivalence. "Take it easy, Rose. It's just dinner. I'm not asking you to negotiate world peace."

My aunt's words came drifting back to me—*You've*

resigned yourself to a lifetime of devotion to your daughter. Don't you realize you're putting the same pressure on her that you believe your father put on you?

I pulled myself together and looked him square in the eye. "Okay, Sheriff. When did you have in mind?" My poor aunt probably didn't expect her words to nudge me into a date with a werewolf. Sheriff Nash was definitely on her Do Not Do Him list.

"Any night that works for you," he said. "And if there's a place you haven't been yet that you'd like to try, let me know."

"I've only been to a handful of places so far," I admitted. "I'll leave the choice to you."

He whistled. "Already leaving me to play the alpha. I'm liking you more every day, Rose."

"Don't get used to it," I said. "I don't abdicate all my decisions. Just the ones I'm less bothered about."

He flashed his lopsided grin. "Noted."

"Thanks for driving me home, Sheriff," I said.

"Your aunt's gonna lose her wand over this," he said. "You know that, right?"

"I made it clear to my aunt that she has no role in my dating life," I said. "She told me I was stubborn like my father."

He chuckled. "I'll text you with the details. That okay?"

I gave him a thumbs up. "I'll be waiting with bated breath."

"If you're gonna do that, you might try a little mouthwash," he said. "I prefer mint flavor myself."

Before I could say another word, he turned and ambled down the walkway back to his patrol car.

I stared after him, wondering what on earth I was getting myself into. A date with Sheriff Nash. Maybe the parasite had infected me differently. Instead of inducing living nightmares, it caused me to make unwise decisions.

The door behind me flew open and Marley stood there, holding a struggling PP3.

"He's less than thrilled," she said, "but I think it's great."

"It's only dinner," I said. "It's not like he's your new father."

"I know," Marley said. "I'm still holding out hope for Alec on that front."

I balked. "You're what? You're angling for your new dad to be a vampire?"

"I like the sheriff, but I really like Alec." She paused. "And I think he really likes you."

I wasn't about to reveal my candid conversations with Alec. Although I tended to overshare, even I had boundaries when it came to my daughter.

"I'm sorry, but Alec isn't an option," I said simply.

"Not now, but he will be."

I glanced at her sharply. "You sound awfully sure for someone with zero clairvoyant ability."

Marley shrugged. "Maybe that'll be the psychic skill I have that you don't."

"Well, you don't have it now," I said. "You're only ten. Another year to go."

"Less than a year," she said proudly. "How will you break the news to Alec?"

"What news? Dinner with the sheriff isn't news."

"If you say so." She carried PP3 back into the house and I trailed behind them, doing my best to ignore the butterflies zooming around in my stomach.

CHAPTER 19

THE NEXT AFTERNOON Marley and I stood on a dock at Balefire Beach, admiring The Laughing Princess.

"I can't believe you got the boat," I said. For all my aunt's intimidation tactics, she truly was a pushover.

"Mother has a hard time denying me things," Florian said, flashing a winning smile.

"And she's not doing you any favors," I said. "No wonder you're stuck in a Peter Pan state. If you don't *have* to grow up, why would you?" As someone who was forced to grow up fast, I knew I wouldn't. I'd cling to a childlike state like plastic wrap.

"To be fair, you did follow through with your end of the deal," Marley said. "You volunteered like she wanted."

"And I'm enjoying it," Florian said. "I'm going to keep working at the tourism board office. Aster seems to have come around to the idea of me being underfoot."

"Don't misjudge her," I said. "She's happy to see you take an interest in something besides glitter. And the boat's a real beauty." Although I knew nothing about boats, this one looked pretty good from the dock.

189

"Would you like to go for a ride?" he asked.

"Yes, please," Marley exclaimed, bouncing up and down.

"I think that's a yes," I said wryly.

"Come aboard," he said.

"Are you sure?" I asked. "It's going to be dark soon."

"All the better," Florian said. "You can't beat the sunset from a boat."

We climbed aboard and I enthused over the luxurious interior. "I think I could get used to this." I leaned on the edge and gazed at the horizon.

"The ocean is in our blood," he said.

"Is it?" I queried. The wind whipped through my hair and I immediately regretted the absence of a baseball hat. One of these days, I was going to master a spell that kept my wayward hair in place.

"Water, wind, sun," he said. "And, soon enough, the moon. All places we draw our magical energy from."

"I hadn't thought about it that way," I said.

I joined Marley on the starboard side of the boat, as Florian called it.

"How's this?" I asked, and Marley's huge smile answered my question.

"We're so lucky, Mom," she said.

"I guess we are."

She glanced up at me. "You guess?"

I didn't want to tell her what I'd been thinking. That life was complicated. That even though I was grateful for so much, I still had regrets about all that I'd lost. That we'd lost.

"You're right," I said finally. "We are very lucky."

The boat began to move and I enjoyed the subtle undulations. I felt like we were gliding on air.

Florian appeared beside us. "Mother asked me to deliver this to you." He handed me a thick book. The rich brown leather of the book was well worn. I brought it to my nose and inhaled the scent.

"Pictures?" I inquired.

He gave a crisp nod.

Marley peered around me, eager to see. I flipped open to the first page and my breath caught in my throat. The first image was of my mother in her silver wedding dress. She held a bouquet of roses.

"She was so pretty," Marley said.

The tip of a wand appeared and Florian gently tapped the photograph. My mother's image sprang to life. She spoke to someone I couldn't see and then laughed at the response.

Marley gasped. "Her laugh sounds like yours."

It did. An odd sound stuck between a cackle and a guffaw. No wonder my father loved to hear my strange laugh. It must have reminded him of his beloved wife.

"Can you animate all the photos?" I asked.

"I can show you and then you can do it yourself," Florian said. "That way you can look through them in your own time."

I nodded, too overcome with emotion to speak.

"Aunt Hyacinth kept these in an album all these years?" Marley asked.

Florian shrugged. "That seems to be the case. She's never shown them to me, so I don't know where she's been hiding them."

"In a place as massive as Thornhold?" I said. "She has about a thousand options for hiding spots. Not to mention a concealment spell."

"Now you're thinking like a witch," Florian said, tapping his temple.

"Maybe we'll see Captain Blackfang while we're sailing the high seas," Marley said excitedly.

"I wouldn't hope for that," Florian said. "Not many survive a run-in with him."

Marley looked downright giddy. The vampire pirate was nothing but a story to her, but I shivered because I knew better.

"Can we sail past the Whitethorn?" she asked. "I want to see if it looks spooky from the water."

"Technically, we don't sail because it's not a sailboat," he said. "But I guarantee you that everything looks amazing from the water."

I didn't disagree. We rode parallel to the coastline, where I observed the twinkling lights of Starry Hollow. The Lighthouse was easy to spot, as it should be. Fairy Cove. Balefire Beach.

"Do you think we'll see the mermaid?" Marley asked. Ever since I'd told her about my kayaking experience, she'd been determined to catch a glimpse of a real-life Ariel.

"There's more than one mermaid," Florian said. "And this time of day is pretty good for spotting one in the water. They're drawn to sunsets same as we are."

Marley squealed with delight and cast her eagle eyes over the ocean. The slightest movement in the water had her gasping for breath.

"Dolphins," I cried. Okay, not as cool as mermaids, but still. I pointed to the six torpedo-shaped bodies swimming in the distance.

Marley's expression was priceless. She'd never seen a dolphin before, let alone six of them.

Suddenly she gripped my hand and squeezed. "I see one."

She didn't need to define *one*. I knew exactly what she meant. I followed her gaze to a spot behind the dolphins. A green tail splashed in the waves before disappearing. A moment later, a brown head emerged.

"A merman," Marley yelled.

"So it is," I said.

He waved to us and we waved back.

"Looks like Lewis," Florian said. "Nice guy. He shot pool at my house a few times."

I inhaled the salty air. I now lived in a place where mermen played pool with my cousin in his mansion. What a world.

We waited until the deep orange and yellow of the sunset faded from the sky before returning to the dock. As much as I enjoyed being on the open water, I couldn't wait to get back to Rose Cottage with Marley to crack open the photo album. A glass of wine, a crackling fire, and a trip down a lane I had no memory of.

I stared into the darkness, perfectly content. The moon glowed like a large silver coin on the blacktop.

It promised to be a perfect evening.

Thank you for reading *Magic & Mischief*! If you enjoyed it, please help other readers find this book so they can enjoy the world of Starry Hollow, too ~

1. Write a review and post it on Amazon.

2. Sign up for my new releases via e-mail here http://eepurl.com/ctYNzf or like me on Facebook so you can find out about the next book before it's even available.

3. Look out for *Magic & Mayhem*, the next book in the series!

4. Other books by Annabel Chase include the **Spellbound** paranormal cozy mystery series.

Curse the Day, Book 1

Doom and Broom, Book 2

Spell's Bells, Book 3

Lucky Charm, Book 4

Better Than Hex, Book 5

Cast Away, Book 6

A Touch of Magic, Book 7

A Drop in the Potion, Book 8

Hemlocked and Loaded, Book 9

All Spell Breaks Loose, Book 10

Spellbound Ever After

Crazy For Brew, Book 1

Lost That Coven Feeling, Book 2

Wands Upon A Time, Book 3

Charmed Offensive, Book 4

Federal Bureau of Magic

Great Balls of Fury, Book 1

Fury Godmother, Book 2

No Guts, No Fury, Book 3

Printed in Poland
by Amazon Fulfillment
Poland Sp. z o.o., Wrocław